I have edited Clive Gilson's books for over a decade now – he's prolific and can turn his hand to many genres - poetry, short fiction, contemporary novels, folklore and science fiction – and the common theme is that none of them ever fails to take my breath away. There's something in each story that is either memorably poignant, hauntingly unnerving or sidesplittingly funny.

Lorna Howarth, *The Write Factor*

Tales From The World's Firesides is a grand project. I've collected thousands of traditional texts as part of other projects, and while many of the original texts are available through channels like Project Gutenberg, some of the narratives can be hard to read for modern audiences, and so the Fireside project was born. Put simply, I collect, collate and adapt traditional tales from around the world and publish them as a modern archive.

This is the very first book in *Part 3 – Africa*, following on from the titles in *Parts 1* and *2* covering a host of nations and regions across Europe and North America.

I'm not laying any claim to insight or specialist knowledge, but these collections are born out of my love of story-telling and I hope that you'll share my affection for traditional tales, myths and legends.

Images by Astrid Schmid and Mohamed Hassan from Pixabay

Arokin Tales

-

Folklore, Fairy Tales and Legends from West Africa

Compiled & Edited by Clive Gilson

Tales from the World's Firesides

Book 1 in Part 3 of the series: Africa

Arokin Tales, edited by Clive Gilson, Solitude, Bath, UK

www.boyonabench.com

First published as an eBook in 2021

This edition © 2021 Clive Gilson

Printed by IngramSpark

ISBN: 978-1-913500-42-9

SOLITUDE

Contents

PREFACE

Africa is, of course, wildly diverse in every aspect, and African culture and storytelling reflects that diversity. Whether you look at creation and flood myths, or at the wonderful tales rooted in animism, these stories are always a delight.

Folktales reflect a group cultural identity and storytelling affirms pride and identity in a culture, and for those of us for whom Africa is a foreign land, these stories provide an insight into community beliefs, views, and customs. For people within those communities, storytelling allows them to encompass and express their group's uniqueness.

As with so many cultures, folktales are also seen as a tool for education and entertainment. They provide a way for children to understand the world around them and their place within it. Most stories here have a moral, and are often set in fantastic, non-human worlds. The main characters in many of these stories are talking animals, reflecting close relationships with nature, and even though folktales are for often told for entertainment, they also bring a sense of belonging and pride to communities in Africa.

Animal tales are often more oriented towards entertainment, but still have morals and lessons to them. Animal tales are normally divided into trickster tales and ogre tales. In the animal tales, a certain animal would always have the same character or role in each story so the audience does not have to worry about characterization. The Hare was always the trickster, clever and cunning, while the Hyena was always being tricked by the Hare. Ogres are always cruel, greedy monsters.

Day-to-Day tales are the most serious tales designed to explain the everyday life and struggles of the community. These tales take on matters such as famine, escape from death, courtship, and family matters, sometimes using a song form when they reach their climax.

Some of these themes are also prevalent in traditional religious beliefs. Animism, for example, facilitates many of the core concepts of traditional African religions, including the worship of tutelary deities, nature worship, ancestor worship and the belief in an afterlife. While some religions adopted a pantheistic worldview, most follow a polytheistic system with various gods, spirits and other supernatural beings. Many traditional African religions also have elements of fetishism, shamanism and veneration of relics.

Traditional African religions can be broken down into linguistic cultural groups, with common themes. Among Niger–Congo-speakers is a belief in a creator God, force or higher deity, which is considered by some to be a widespread and ancient feature of Niger-Congo-cultures

Traditional African medicine is also directly linked to traditional African religions and storytelling. The belief in spirits and ancestors is an important element of African religions, where Gods were often self-created or evolved from spirits or ancestors. That being said, in more recent years it is also true that African folk religions were strongly influenced by non-African religions, mostly Christianity and Islam and have, therefore, evolved and may differ from the more ancient forms.

However expressed it remains important that ancestral ghosts and spirits are an integral part of reality. The ancestors are generally believed to reside in an ancestral realm or spirit world, while some believe that the ancestors became equal in power to deities.

The defining line between deities and ancestors is often contested, but overall, ancestors are believed to occupy a higher level of existence than living human beings and are believed to be able to bestow either blessings or illness upon their living descendants. Ancestors can offer advice and bestow good fortune and honour to their living dependents, but they can also make demands, such as insisting that their shrines be properly maintained and propitiated. A belief in ancestors also testifies to the inclusive nature of traditional African spirituality by positing that deceased progenitors still play a role in the lives of their living descendants.

As ever I have been amazed and touched and have fallen in love with yet another body of storytelling. In particular, Tortoise and Anansi have become firm friends this winter.

I do hope you enjoy these stories as much as I have.

Clive

Bath, 2021

THE SLAVE GIRL WHO TRIED TO KILL HER MISTRESS

This story has been edited and adapted from Elphinstone Dayrell's Folk Stories From Southern Nigeria, first published in 1910 by Longmans, Green And Company, London And New York.

A man called Akpan, who was a native of Oku, a town in the Ibibio country, admired a girl called Emme very much. Emme lived at Ibibio and wished to marry her as she was the finest girl in her company. It was the custom in those days for the parents to demand such a large amount for their daughters as dowry, that if after they were married they failed to get on with their husbands, as they could not redeem themselves, they were sold as slaves. Akpan paid a very large sum as dowry for Emme, and she was put in the fatting-house until the proper time arrived for her to marry.

Akpan told the parents that when their daughter was ready they must send her over to him. This they promised to do. Emme's father was a rich man, and after seven years had elapsed, and it became time for her to go to her husband, he saw a very fine girl, who had also just come out of the fatting-house, and whom the parents wished to sell as a slave. Emme's father therefore bought her, and gave her to his daughter as her handmaiden.

The next day Emme's little sister, being very anxious to go with her, obtained the consent of her mother, and they started off together, the slave girl carrying a large bundle containing clothes and presents from Emme's father. Akpan's house was a long day's march from where they lived.

When they arrived just outside the town they came to a spring, where the people used to get their drinking water from, but no one was allowed to bathe there. Emme, however, knew nothing about this. They took off their clothes to wash close to the spring, and where there was a deep hole which led to the Water Ju-Ju's house. The slave girl knew of this Ju-Ju, and thought if she could get her mistress to bathe, she would be taken by the Ju-Ju, and she would then be able to take her place and marry Akpan. So they went down to bathe, and when they were close to the water the slave girl pushed her mistress in, and she at once disappeared.

The little girl then began to cry, but the slave girl said, "If you cry any more I will kill you at once, and throw your body into the hole after your sister." And she told the child that she must never mention what had happened to any one, and particularly not to Akpan, as she was going to represent her sister and marry him, and that if she ever told anyone what she had seen, she would be killed at once. She then made the little girl carry her load to Akpan's house.

When they arrived, Akpan was very much disappointed at the slave girl's appearance, as she was not nearly as pretty and fine as he had expected her to be, but as he had not seen Emme for seven years, he had no suspicion that the girl was not really Emme, for whom he had paid such a large dowry. He then called all his company together to play and feast, and when they arrived they were much astonished, and said, "Is this the fine woman for whom you paid so much dowry, and whom you told us so much about?" And Akpan could not answer them.

The slave girl was very cruel to Emme's little sister, and wanted her to die, so that her position would be more secure with her husband. She beat the little girl every day, and always made her carry the largest water-pot to the spring; she also made the child place her finger in the fire to use as firewood. When the time came for food, the slave girl went to the fire and got a burning piece of wood and burned the child all over the body with it. When Akpan asked her why she treated the child so badly, she replied that she was a slave that her father had bought for her. When the little girl took the heavy water-pot to the river to fill it there was no one to lift it up for her, so that she could not get it on to her head. She therefore had to remain a long time at the spring, and at last began calling for her sister Emme to come and help her.

When Emme heard her little sister crying for her, she begged the Water Ju-Ju to allow her to go and help her, so he told her she might go, but that she must return to him again immediately. When the little girl saw her sister she did not want to leave her, and asked to be allowed to go into the hole with her. She then told Emme how very badly she had been treated by the slave girl, and her elder sister told her to have patience and wait, that a day of vengeance would arrive sooner or later.

The little girl went back to Akpan's house with a glad heart as she had seen her sister, but when she got to the house, the slave girl said, "Why have you been so long getting the water?" and then took another stick from the fire and burnt the little girl again very badly, and starved her for the rest of the day.

This went on for some time, until, one day, when the child went to the river for water, after all the people had gone, she cried out for her sister as usual. She did not come for a long time, as there was a hunter from Akpan's town hidden nearby watching the hole, and the Water Ju-Ju told Emme that she must not go. The little girl went on crying bitterly, and Emme at last persuaded the Ju-Ju to let her go, promising to return quickly. When she emerged from the water, she looked very beautiful with the rays of the setting sun shining on her glistening body. She helped her little sister with her water-pot, and then disappeared into the hole again.

The hunter was amazed at what he had seen, and when he returned, he told Akpan what a beautiful woman had come out of the water and had helped the little girl with her water-pot. He also told Akpan that he was convinced that the girl he had seen at the spring was his proper wife, Emme, and that the Water Ju-Ju must have taken her.

Akpan then made up his mind to go out and watch and see what happened, so, in the early morning the hunter came for him, and they both went down to the river, and hid in the forest near the water-hole.

When Akpan saw Emme come out of the water, he recognised her at once, and went home and considered how he should get her out of the power of the Water Ju-Ju. He was advised by some of his friends to go to an old woman, who frequently made sacrifices to the Water Ju-Ju, and consult her as to what was the best thing to do.

When he went to her, she told him to bring her one white slave, one white goat, one piece of white cloth, one white chicken, and a basket of eggs. Then, when the great Ju-Ju day arrived, she would take them to the Water Ju-Ju, and make a sacrifice of them on his behalf. The day after the sacrifice was made, the Water Ju-Ju would return the girl to her, and she would bring her to Akpan.

Akpan then bought the slave, and took all the other things to the old woman, and, when the day of the sacrifice arrived, he went with his friend the hunter and witnessed the old woman make the sacrifice. The slave was bound up and led to the hole, then the old woman called to the Water Ju-Ju and cut the slave's throat with a sharp knife and pushed him into the hole. She then did the same to the goat and chicken, and also threw the eggs and cloth in on top of them.

After this had been done, they all returned to their homes. The next morning at dawn the old woman went to the hole, and found Emme standing at the side of the spring, so she told her that she was her friend, and was going to take her to her husband. She then took Emme back to her own home, and hid her in her room, and sent word to Akpan to come to her house, and to take great care that the slave woman knew nothing about the matter. So Akpan left the house secretly by the back door, and arrived at the old woman's house without meeting anybody.

When Emme saw Akpan, she asked for her little sister, so he sent his friend, the hunter, to the spring for her, and he met her carrying her water-pot to get the morning supply of water for the house, and he brought her to the old woman's house.

When Emme had embraced her sister, she told her to return to the house and do something to annoy the slave woman, and then she was to run as fast as she could back to the old woman's house, where, no doubt, the slave girl would follow her, and would meet them all inside the house, and see Emme, who she believed she had killed.

The little girl did as she was told, and, directly she got into the house, she called out to the slave woman: "Do you know that you are a wicked woman, and have treated me very badly? I know you are only my sister's slave, and you will be properly punished."

She then ran as hard as she could to the old woman's house. Directly the slave woman heard what the little girl said, she was quite mad with rage, and seized a burning stick from the fire, and ran after the child, but the little one got to the house first, and ran inside, the slave woman following close upon her heels with the burning stick in her hand.

Then Emme came out and confronted the slave woman, and she at once recognised her mistress, whom she thought she had killed, so she stood quite still.

Then they all went back to Akpan's house, and when they arrived there, Akpan asked the slave woman what she meant by pretending that she was Emme, and why she had tried to kill her. But, seeing she was found out, the slave woman had nothing to say.

Many people were then called to a play to celebrate the recovery of Akpan's wife, and when they had all come, he told them what the slave woman had done.

After this, Emme treated the slave girl in the same way as she had treated her little sister. She made her put her fingers in the fire, and burnt her with sticks. She also made her beat foo-foo with her head in a hollowed-out tree, and after a time she was tied up to a tree and starved to death.

Ever since that time, when a man marries a girl, he is always present when she comes out of the fatting-house and takes her home himself, so that such evil things as happened to Emme and her sister may not occur again.

HOW THE SKY-GOD'S STORIES CAME TO BE ANANSI'S STORIES

This story has been edited and adapted from Captain R. S. Rattray's Akan-Ashanti Folk-Tales, first published in 1930 by Oxford University Press – American Branch, New York.

The Sky-God Nyame, who is also known as Nyankonpon, had all of the world's stories. Anansi wanted Nyame's stories so he went to Nyame and asked if he could buy them from him. Nyame did not want to give up his stories, even though the Spider insisted he could afford to pay for them. Unconvinced, Nyame then told Anansi that many great kingdoms like Kokofu, Bekwai, and Asumengya tried to buy the stories from him yet couldn't afford them; he then pondered how Anansi, completely insignificant in comparison, would succeed where they had failed. Anansi, however, was not intimidated and promised he could afford them, asking Nyame their price.

As a result, Nyame entertained Anansi's offer, but nonetheless set a high price, hoping that it would be impossible for Anansi to accomplish the difficult labours that he devised for him: Anansi had to capture four of the most dangerous creatures in the world, namely Onini the Python, the Mmoboro Hornets, Osebo the Leopard, and the Fairy Mmoatia. Undaunted, clever Anansi promised to bring Nyame those four things and even added his own mother Ya Nsia for extra measure. Nyame accepted his offer and advised him to begin his journey, so Anansi set about putting his schemes into motion.

First, Anansi went to his family and told them about his plan, including Ya Nsia. Then, he asked his wife Aso for advice, as he wished to capture Onini the Python first. Aso advised him to cut a branch from a palm tree and gather some string creeper vines. Anansi returned with them, and Aso told him to take them to the river where Onini lived nearby, pretending to argue with her to draw the Python's attention. Anansi agreed with her plan and took them. He then pretended to debate with her in an imaginary argument over the length of Onini's body while he headed there, pretending Aso had claimed Onini's body was longer than the branch of a full-grown palm tree.

Onini eventually heard Anansi pretending to argue with Aso, so he approached the Spider and asked Anansi what he was talking about. Anansi explained and Onini, unaware of Anansi's trickery, quickly agreed to help Anansi prove that he was longer than a palm tree branch. So, Anansi told the Python to stretch himself beside the branch Anansi had gathered and Onini then did so eagerly, unaware he'd fallen into a trap. Anansi then took the string creeper vines he'd gathered and tied up Onini completely. Anansi then lost no time in carrying Onini off to Nyame, mocking the Python along the way as he informed Onini of his bargain with Nyame. Triumphant, Anansi soon arrived and presented Onini to Nyame. the Sky-God acknowledged Anansi's accomplishment but reminded him that he still had the other challenges, imagining in secret that Anansi would fail.

Next, Anansi returned home to Aso and informed her of what he had accomplished, deciding to capture the Mmoboro Hornets next. He asked her for advice, and his wife obliged, telling him to find a gourd and fill it with water. He was then to carry the gourd along with him to see the Hornets.

Anansi followed her advice, heading toward the bush where the Hornets roamed in search of them. Soon, the Spider noticed a swarm of Hornets loitering near a bush, and he crept close to them, readying his gourd. Anansi then sprinkled some of his water at the Mmoboro Hornets, careful to save some for himself. The Spider then doused himself with the remaining water he'd collected and cut a leaf from a Banana tree nearby, covering his head with it. Soon the Hornets flew to him in a fit but Anansi showed them his banana leaf – still wet – and explained that it had been raining. Clever Anansi then warned the Hornets that the rain was dangerous, suggesting that they could enter his gourd so that they wouldn't be overcome.

The Hornets agreed and thanked Anansi for helping them – unaware of his scheme – and they all flew inside, filling the gourd as they sought the shelter Anansi had promised them. Once all of them had entered, Anansi stoppered the mouth of the gourd and taunted them for succumbing to his scheme. The Spider told them of his plan to trade them to the Sky-God for his stories and took the Hornets to Nyame. Nyame accepted the Hornets, but reminded Anansi that he still had other tasks left in spite of his successes so far, certain the Spider still could not complete his task. He bade the Spider to continue his search, and Anansi left for home.

Anansi soon returned to Aso afterward and informed her of his success, then plotted against Osebo the Leopard with her. Aso told Anansi to dig a hole to catch Osebo and cover it; Anansi caught on to her plan immediately and told her it was enough.

Then, he went to the place where Osebo could normally be found. Anansi dug a deep pit in the ground, covered it with brushwood, and decided to return home, knowing that Osebo would eventually stumble into the pit as night drew near. Sure enough, Anansi returned to the pit the next morning and found Osebo trapped inside of it.

Anansi feigned sympathy and asked the Leopard why he was trapped inside. He asked Osebo if he'd been drinking again, something Anansi had constantly warned the Leopard about, and the Spider continued his act, lamenting that he wanted to help Osebo but was certain that Osebo would attempt to eat him afterward. Osebo insisted that he wouldn't harm Anansi, so the Spider agreed to help him.

Anansi went aside and cut two long sticks with his knife for the Leopard to climb out of the hole with and told Osebo to stretch his arms wide, secretly leaving the Leopard vulnerable. Osebo, unaware of yet another scheme by Anansi, then attempted to scale the sticks so that he could escape, but Anansi withdrew his knife again and tossed it at Osebo. The hilt of the knife struck Osebo's head and the Leopard fell down into the pit, now unconscious.

Satisfied that his scheme had worked, Anansi gathered some additional sticks and formed a ladder, descending to the bottom of the pit to collect Osebo. Anansi then gloated just as he had before and told the Leopard about his bargain with Nyame, carrying him away to the Sky-God. Anansi then presented Osebo to Nyame when he arrived, and Nyame accepted Anansi's gift. The Sky-God, however, was still not convinced that Anansi would succeed in completing his challenge, and reminded the Spider that he had yet to accomplish all of the tasks he was assigned.

The Spider returned home another time, deciding to capture Mmoatia the Fairy after some thought. Anansi then decided upon a plan and carved an Akua doll. Next, the Spider gathered the sap out of a gum tree, covering it until the Akua doll thus became very sticky, but Anansi was not done. He pounded some eto (mashed yams) collected by his wife Aso and covered the Akua doll's hand with it; the Spider then gathered a basin and placed some eto inside of it. Once he'd filled the basin, Anansi then took some of his silk and tied a string around the Akua doll's waist so that he could manipulate it, heading off to the land of fairies once he'd finished.

Anansi placed the doll in front of an odum tree, a place where Fairies often congregated, and sat the basin with the eto in front of it as bait. Anansi then hid behind the odum tree and waited for one of the Mmoatia to appear. Soon, one came, lured away from her sisters by the eto that the Spider had placed in front of the Akua doll. Enticed by the eto, Mmoatia asked the doll if she could have some of it. Anansi then tugged the Akua doll's waist and it nodded its head in response, which made Mmoatia excited. Mmoatia returned to her sisters and asked if they'd allow her to eat some, noting that she, completely unaware of Anansi's trickery, had been offered some eto by the Akua doll.

Mmoatia's sisters allowed her to, so the Fairy returned to the basin and devoured the eto. When she'd finished, Mmoatia thanked the Akua doll but Anansi did not tug his string. The Akua doll did not nod to acknowledge Mmoatia's gratitude. Slightly upset, Mmoatia told her sisters what had happened and they advised her to slap the doll's face as recompense. Mmoatia agreed and then slapped the Akua doll, but her hand became stuck.

Angered, the Fairy informed them of what had happened, and another sister suggested that Mmoatia should slap the doll again, this time with her other hand. The Fairy obliged and tried again, only for her remaining hand to become stuck on the gum that covered the Akua doll.

Mmoatia asked her sisters for help a final time, informing them that both her hands were now stuck. Another sister told Mmoatia to bludgeon the doll with the rest of her body, certain that Mmoatia would be successful this time in punishing the Akua doll. However, the Fairy followed the advice of her sisters and only became entirely stuck to the gum that covered the doll Anansi had laid in front of the Odum tree.

Anansi then emerged from hiding and used the rest of the string he'd tied around his doll to bind Mmoatia with his string entirely. He then mocked Mmoatia also, just as he had done to the others he'd captured before her and told the Fairy of his scheme to offer her to Nyame as well. However, Anansi still had another task he wished to complete before he returned to the Sky-God.

Finally, Anansi headed to his home to visit his mother Ya Nsia, and reminded her of his agreement with the Sky-God to exchange her as part of the price for Nyame's stories. Anansi's mother complied with him, and the Spider then carried her alongside Mmoatia to Nyame, presenting both of them to Nyame to complete the bargain for the Sky-God's stories. Nyame accepted both of them, thoroughly-impressed at the success of the Spider, and assembled a meeting within his kingdom. The Sky-God summoned his elders, the Kontire and Akwam chiefs, the Adontem general of his army's main body, the Gyase, the Oyoko, Ankobea, and finally Kyidom, who led his rear-guard.

Nyame then told them about the task Anansi had accomplished when none else, not even the greatest kingdoms, could afford his stories. Nyame recounted each of the creatures Anansi had presented the Sky-God with, as well as his own mother Ya Nsia, and allowed his audience to see each of these gifts for themselves. Nyame finally acknowledged Anansi's talents and told the Spider he now had the Sky-God's blessings. The people rejoiced alongside Nyame as he then announced that his stories would no longer be known by his name or belong to him. From then on, the Sky-God's stories would belong to Anansi, and all of them would be known as Spider stories for eternity. So it is that every story, no matter the subject or theme, is called a Spider story.

ANANSI AND THE DISPERSAL OF WISDOM

This story has been edited and adapted from Captain R. S. Rattray's Akan-Ashanti Folk-Tales, first published in 1930 by Oxford University Press – American Branch, New York.

Anansi was already very clever, but he wanted more knowledge, so he decided to gather all the wisdom that he could find and keep it in a safe place. Soon Anansi collected all of the wisdom found throughout the world and sealed it all inside of a pot.

However, he was still concerned that it was not safe enough, so he secretly took the pot to a tall thorny tree in the forest. His younger son, Ntikuma, saw him go and followed him at some distance to see what he was doing. Ntikuma noticed the pot was much bigger than Anansi could handle and he couldn't hold it while trying to climb the tree. As a result, Anansi tied the pot in front of him and then resumed his attempt. Yet, the pot still obscured Anansi and caused him to slip down the tree as he climbed. Each failure caused Anansi to become increasingly frustrated.

Ntikuma laughed when he saw what Anansi was doing. "Why don't you tie the pot behind you, then you will be able to grip the tree?" he suggested.

Anansi was so annoyed by his failed attempts and the realization that his child was right that the pot slipped from his possession. The pot soon crashed into the ground, and all of the wisdom that the Spider had stored inside of it spilled out of it. To make matters even worse, a storm arrived and caused a mighty rain throughout the forest. The deluge of rainwater covered the ground and washed the wisdom that had spilled away from them, until it washed into the river stream nearby. The currents of the stream carried the wisdom Anansi had collected out to sea, and soon it spread throughout the entire world, ruining Anansi's plan and making his goal impossible. This angered the Spider.

Anansi then chased his son Ntikuma home throughout the rain, but he soon came to an epiphany and accepted his loss once he finally caught up with his son.

"What is the use of all that wisdom if a young child still needs to put you right?"

Thus, Anansi failed to steal the world's wisdom that day, and instead, a little of it lives in everyone.

A QUESTION AS TO AGE

This story has been edited and adapted from Robert Hamill Nassau's Where Animals Talk, first published in 1912 by Richard G. Badger at The Gorham Press, based out of Boston. This tale was originally told by storytellers from the Fang tribe.

Shrike was a blacksmith. So, all the Beasts went to the forge at his town. Each day, when they had finished at the anvil, they took all their tools and laid them on the ground as pledges. Before they should go back to their towns, they would say to the Bird, "Show us which is the eldest, and then you give us the things, if you are able to decide our question."

Shrike looked at and examined them, but he did not know, for they were all apparently of the same age, and they went away empty-handed, leaving their tools as a challenge. Every day it was that same way.

On another day, Tortoise, being a friend of the Bird, started to go to work for him at the bellows. Also, he cooked three bundles of food; one of Civet with the entrails of a red Antelope, and one of Genet, and one of an Edubu-Snake. Then he blew at the bellows.

When the others were hungry at meal time, Tortoise took up the jomba-bundles, and he said, "Come on, you venerable ones! Take up this jomba of Njâbâ with the entrails, and eat."

Again Tortoise said, "Come on youngsters! Take up the jomba of Uhingi."

He then took up the jomba of the Snake. And he said, "Come on, my children! Take of the jomba of Edubu."

After a while they all finished their work at the bellows. They still left their tools lying on the ground, and came near to the Bird, and they said, as on other occasions, "Show us who is the eldest."

Then Tortoise at the request of the Bird, announced the decision, as if it was its own, "You who ate of the Njâbâ are the ones who are oldest; you who ate of Uhingi are the ones who are younger men, and you who ate of the Edubu are the ones who are the youngest."

So, they assented to the decision, and took away their belongings.

ANANZI AND BABOON

This story has been edited and adapted from the appendix of George Webbe Dasent's Popular Tales From The Norse, first published in 1907 by Edmonston and Douglas, based out of Edinburgh, Scotland.

Anansi and Baboon were disputing one day which was fattest. Anansi said he was sure he was fat, but Baboon declared he was fatter. Then Anansi proposed that they should prove it; so they made a fire, and agreed that they should hang up before it, and see which would drop most fat.

Then Baboon hung up Anansi first, but no fat dropped.

Then Anansi hung up Baboon, and very soon the fat began to drop, which smelt so good that Anansi cut a slice out of Baboon, and said, "Oh, brother Baboon, you're fat for true."

But Baboon didn't speak.

So Anansi said, "Well, speak or not speak, I'll eat you every bit to- day", which he really did. But when he had eaten up all of Baboon, the bits joined themselves together in his stomach, and began to pull him about so much that he had no rest, and was obliged to go to a doctor.

The doctor told him not to eat anything for some days, then he was to get a ripe banana, and hold it to his mouth; when the Baboon, who would be hungry, smelt the banana, he would be sure to run up to eat it, and so he would run out of his mouth.

So Anansi starved himself, and got the banana, and did as the doctor told him, but when he put the banana to his mouth, he was so hungry he couldn't help eating it. So he didn't get rid of the Baboon, which went on pulling him about till he was obliged to go back to the doctor, who told him he would soon cure him, and he took the banana, and held it to Anansi's mouth, and very soon the Baboon jumped up to catch it, and ran out of his mouth, and Anansi was very glad to get rid of him. And Baboons to this very day like bananas..

CONCERNING THE FATE OF ESSIDO AND HIS EVIL COMPANIONS

This story has been edited and adapted from Elphinstone Dayrell's Folk Stories From Southern Nigeria, first published in 1910 by Longmans, Green And Company, London And New York.

Chief Oborri lived at a town called Adiagor, which is on the right bank of the Calabar River. He was a wealthy chief, and belonged to the Egbo Society. He had many large canoes, and plenty of slaves to paddle them. These canoes he used to fill up with new yams, each canoe being under one head slave and containing eight paddles; the canoes were capable of holding three puncheons of palm-oil, and cost eight hundred rods each. When they were full, about ten of them used to start off together and paddle to Rio del Rey. They went through creeks all the way, which run through mangrove swamps, with palm-oil trees here and there.

Sometimes in the tornado season it was very dangerous crossing the creeks, as the canoes were so heavily laden, having only a few inches above the water, that quite a small wave would fill the canoe and cause it to sink to the bottom. Although most of the boys could swim, it often happened that some of them were lost, as there are many large alligators in these waters. After four days' hard paddling they would arrive at Rio del Rey, where they had very little difficulty in exchanging their new yams for bags of dried shrimps and sticks with smoked fish on them.

Chief Oborri had two sons, named Eyo and Essido. Their mother having died when they were babies, the children were brought up by their father. As they grew up, they developed entirely different characters. The eldest was very hard-working and led a solitary life, but the younger son was fond of gaiety and was very lazy, in fact, he spent most of his time in the neighbouring towns playing and dancing. When the two boys arrived at the respective ages of eighteen and twenty their father died, and they were left to look after themselves. According to native custom, the elder son, Eyo, was entitled to the whole of his father's estate, but being very fond of his younger brother, he gave him a large number of rods and some land with a house. Immediately Essido became possessed of the money he became wilder than ever, gave big feasts to his companions, and always had his house full of women, upon whom he spent large sums. Although the amount his brother had given him on his father's death was very large, in the course of a few years Essido had spent it all. He then sold his house and effects, and spent the proceeds on feasting.

While he had been living this gay and unprofitable life, Eyo had been working harder than ever at his father's old trade, and had made many trips to Rio del Rey himself. Almost every week he had canoes laden with yams going down river and returning after about twelve days with shrimps and fish, which Eyo himself disposed of in the neighbouring markets, and he very rapidly became a rich man. At intervals he remonstrated with Essido on his extravagance, but his warnings had no effect; if anything, his brother became worse.

At last the time arrived when all his money was spent, so Essido went to his brother and asked him to lend him two thousand rods, but Eyo refused, and told Essido that he would not help him in any way to continue his present life of debauchery, but that if he liked to work on the farm and trade, he would give him a fair share of the profits. This Essido indignantly refused, and went back to the town and consulted some of the very few friends he had left as to what was the best thing to do.

The men he spoke to were thoroughly bad men, and had been living upon Essido for a long time. They suggested to him that he should go round the town and borrow money from the people he had entertained, and then they would run away to Akpabryos town, which was about four days' march from Calabar. This Essido did, and managed to borrow a lot of money, although many people refused to lend him anything. Then at night he set off with his evil companions, who carried his money, as they had not been able to borrow any themselves, being so well known.

When they arrived at Akpabryos town they found many beautiful women and graceful dancers. They then started the same life again, until after a few weeks most of the money had gone. They then met and consulted together how to get more money, and advised Essido to return to his rich brother, pretending that he was going to work and give up his old life; he should then get poison from a man they knew of, and place it in his brother's food, so that he would die, and then Essido would become possessed of all his brother's wealth, and they would be able to live in the same way as they had formerly.

Essido, who had sunk very low, agreed to this plan, and they left Akpabryos town the next morning. After marching for two days, they arrived at a small hut in the bush where a man who was an expert poisoner lived, called Okponesip. He was the head Ju-Ju man of the country, and when they had bribed him with eight hundred rods he swore them to secrecy, and gave Essido a small parcel containing a deadly poison which he said would kill his brother in three months. All he had to do was to place the poison in his brother's food.

When Essido returned to his brother's house he pretended to be very sorry for his former mode of living, and said that for the future he was going to work. Eyo was very glad when he heard this, and at once asked his brother in, and gave him new clothes and plenty to eat.

In the evening, when supper was being prepared, Essido went into the kitchen, pretending he wanted to get a light from the fire for his pipe. The cook being absent and no one about, he put the poison in the soup, and then returned to the living-room. He then asked for some tombo, which was brought, and when he had finished it, he said he did not want any supper, and went to sleep. His brother, Eyo, had supper by himself and consumed all the soup. In a week's time he began to feel very ill, and as the days passed he became worse, so he sent for his Ju-Ju man.

When Essido saw him coming, he quietly left the house, but the Ju-Ju man, by casting lots, very soon discovered that it was Essido who had given poison to his brother. When he told Eyo this, he would not believe it, and sent him away. However, when Essido returned, his elder brother told him what the Ju-Ju man had said, but that he did not believe him for one moment, and had sent him away. Essido was much relieved when he heard this, but as he was anxious that no suspicion of the crime should be attached to him, he went to the Household Ju-Ju, and having first sworn that he had never administered poison to his brother, he drank out of the pot.

Three months after he had taken the poison Eyo died, much to the grief of every one who knew him, as he was much respected, not only on account of his great wealth, but because he was also an upright and honest man, who never did harm to anyone.

Essido kept his brother's funeral according to the usual custom, and there was much playing and dancing, which was kept up for a long time. Then Essido paid off his old creditors in order to make himself popular, and kept open house, entertaining most lavishly, and spending his money in many foolish ways. All the bad women about collected at his house, and his old evil companions went on as they had done before.

Things got so bad that none of the respectable people would have anything to do with him, and at last the chiefs of the country, seeing the way Essido was squandering his late brother's estate, assembled together, and eventually came to the conclusion that he was a witch man, and had poisoned his brother in order to acquire his position. The chiefs, who were all friends of the late Eyo, and who were very sorry at his death, as they knew that if he had lived he would have become a great and powerful chief, made up their minds to give Essido the Ekpawor Ju-Ju, which is a very strong medicine, and gets into men's heads, so that when they have drunk it they are compelled to speak the truth, and if they have done wrong they die very shortly.

Essido was then told to dress himself and attend the meeting at the palaver house, and when he arrived the chiefs charged him with having killed his brother by witchcraft. Essido denied having done so, but the chiefs told him that if he were innocent he must prove it by drinking the bowl of Ekpawor medicine which was placed before him. As he could not refuse to drink, he drank the bowl off in great fear and trembling, and very soon the Ju-Ju having got hold of him, he confessed that he had poisoned his brother, but that his friends had advised him to do so. About two hours after drinking the Ekpawor, Essido died in great pain.

The friends were then brought to the meeting and tied up to posts, and questioned as to the part they had taken in the death of Eyo. As they were too frightened to answer, the chiefs told them that they knew from Essido that they had induced him to poison his brother. They were then taken to the place where Eyo was buried. The grave had been dug open, and their heads were cut off and fell into the grave, and their bodies were thrown in after them as a sacrifice for the wrong they had done. The grave was then filled up again.

Ever since that time, whenever anyone is suspected of being a witch, he is tried by the Ekpawor Ju-Ju.

ANANZI AND QUANQUA

This story has been edited and adapted from the appendix of George Webbe Dasent's Popular Tales From The Norse, first published in 1907 by Edmonston and Douglas, based out of Edinburgh, Scotland.

Quanqua was a very clever fellow, and he had a large house full of all sorts of meat. But you must know he had a way of saying Quan? qua? (how? what?) when any one asked him anything and so they called him 'Quanqua'.

One day when he was out, he met Atoukama, Anansi's wife, who was going along driving an ox, but the ox would not walk, so Atoukama asked Quanqua to help her, and they got on pretty well, till they came to a river, when the ox would not cross through the water. Then Atoukama called to Quanqua to drive the ox across, but all she could get out of him was, "QUAN? QUA? Quan? Qua?"

At last she said, "Oh! You stupid fellow, you're no good; stop here and mind the ox while I go and get help to drive him across."

So off she went to fetch Anansi. As soon as Atoukama was gone away, Quanqua killed the ox, and hid it all away, where Anansi should not see it, but first he cut off the tail, then he dug a hole near the river side and stuck the tail partly in, leaving out the tip. When he saw Anansi coming, he caught hold of the tail, pretending to tug at it as if he were pulling the ox out of the hole. Anansi seeing this, ran up as fast as he could, and tugging at the tail with all his might, fell over into the river, but he still had hold of the tail, and contrived to get across the water.

Then he called out to Quanqua, "You idle fellow, you couldn't take care of the ox, so you shan't have a bit of the tail", and then on he went. When he was gone quite out of sight, Quanqua took the ox home, and made a very good dinner.

Next day he went to Anansi's house, and said, Anansi must give him some of the tail, for he had got plenty of yams, but he had no meat. Then they agreed to cook their pot together. Quanqua was to put in white yams, and Anansi the tail, and red yams. When they came to put the yams in, Quanqua put in a great many white yams, but Anansi only put in one little red cush-cush yam. Quanqua asked him if that little yam would be enough, and Anansi said, "Oh! Plenty, for I don't eat much."

When the pot boiled, they uncovered it, and sat down to eat their shares, but they couldn't find any white yams at all because the little red one had turned them all red. So Anansi claimed them all, and Quanqua was glad to take what Anansi would give him.

Now, when they had done eating, they said they would try to find out which of them could bear heat best, so they heated two irons, and Anansi was to try first on Quanqua, but he made so many attempts, that the iron got cold before he got near him. Then it was Quanqua's turn, and he pulled the iron out of the fire, and poked it right down Anansi's throat.

A QUESTION OF RIGHT OF INHERITANCE

This story has been edited and adapted from Robert Hamill Nassau's Where Animals Talk, first published in 1912 by Richard G. Badger at The Gorham Press, based out of Boston. This tale was originally told by storytellers from the Fang tribe.

Parrot and Sparrow argued about their right to inherit the property that a Man had left.

The Sparrow said, "The Man and I lived all our days in the same town. If he moved, I also moved. Our interests were similar. At whatever place he went to live, then I stood in the street there as well."

The Parrot spoke, and based his claim on the grounds that he was the original cause of the Man's wealth. He said, "I was born in the tree-tops. Then the Man came and took me to live with him. When my tail began to grow, he and his people took my feathers, with which they made a handsome head-dress. They sold the head-dress for very many goods, with which they bought a wife. And that woman bore daughters, who, for much money, were sold into marriages. Their children also bore other children, and for that reason I say that I was the foundation of all this wealth."

This was what Parrot declared.

So, the people decided, "Koho, the parrot, is the source of those things." And he was allowed to inherit.

HOW THE TORTOISE OVERCAME THE ELEPHANT AND THE HIPPOPOTAMUS

This story has been edited and adapted from Elphinstone Dayrell's Folk Stories From Southern Nigeria, first published in 1910 by Longmans, Green And Company, London And New York.

The elephant and the hippopotamus always used to feed together, and were good friends. One day when they were both dining together, the tortoise appeared and said that although they were both big and strong, neither of them could pull him out of the water with a strong piece of tie-tie, and he offered the elephant ten thousand rods if he could draw him out of the river the next day.

The elephant, seeing that the tortoise was very small, said, "If I cannot draw you out of the water, I will give you twenty thousand rods."

So on the following morning the tortoise got some very strong tie-tie and made it fast to his leg, and went down to the river. When he got there, as he knew the place well, he made the tie-tie fast round a big rock, and left the other end on the shore for the elephant to pull by, then went down to the bottom of the river and hid himself. The elephant then came down and started pulling, and after a time he smashed the rope.

Directly this happened, the tortoise undid the rope from the rock and came to the land, showing all people that the rope was still fast to his leg, but that the elephant had failed to pull him out. The elephant was thus forced to admit that the tortoise was the winner, and paid to him the twenty thousand rods, as agreed. The tortoise then took the rods home to his wife, and they lived together very happily.

After three months had passed, the tortoise, seeing that the money was greatly reduced, thought he would make some more by the same trick, so he went to the hippopotamus and made the same bet with him.

The hippopotamus said, "I will make the bet, but I shall take the water and you shall take the land; I will then pull you into the water."

To this the tortoise agreed, so they went down to the river as before, and having got some strong tie-tie, the tortoise made it fast to the hippopotamus' hind leg, and told him to go into the water. Directly the hippo had turned his back and disappeared, the tortoise took the rope twice round a strong palm-tree which was growing near, and then hid himself at the foot of the tree.

When the hippo was tired of pulling, he came up puffing and blowing water into the air from his nostrils. Directly the tortoise saw him coming up, he unwound the rope, and walked down towards the hippopotamus, showing him the tie-tie round his leg. The hippo had to acknowledge that the tortoise was too strong for him, and reluctantly handed over the twenty thousand rods.

The elephant and the hippo then agreed that they would take the tortoise as their friend, as he was so very strong, but he was not really so strong as they thought, and had won because he was so cunning.

He then told them that he would like to live with both of them, but that, as he could not be in two places at the same time, he said that he would leave his son to live with the elephant on the land, and that he himself would live with the hippopotamus in the water.

This explains why there are both tortoises on the land and tortoises who live in the water. The water tortoise is always much the bigger of the two, as there is plenty of fish for him to eat in the river, whereas the land tortoise is often very short of food.

ANANZI AND THE LION

This story has been edited and adapted from the appendix of George Webbe Dasent's Popular Tales From The Norse, first published in 1907 by Edmonston and Douglas, based out of Edinburgh, Scotland.

Once on a time Anansi planned a scheme. He went to town and bought ever so many firkins of fat, and ever so many sacks, and ever so many balls of string, and a very big frying pan, then he went to the bay and blew a shell, and called the Head-fish in the sea, Green Eel, to him.

Then he said to the fish, "The King sends me to tell you that you must bring all the fish on shore, for he wants to give them new life."

So Green Eel said he would, and went to call them. Meanwhile Anansi lighted a fire, and took out some of the fat, and got his frying pan ready, and as fast as the fish came out of the water he caught them and put them into the frying pan, and so he did with all of them until he got to the Head-fish, who was so slippery that he couldn't hold him, and he got back again into the water.

When Anansi had fried all, the fish, he put them into the sacks, and took the sacks on his back and set off to the mountains. He had not gone very far when he met Lion, and Lion said to him, "Well, brother Anansi, where have you been? I have not seen you a long time."

Anansi said, "I have been travelling about."

"But what have you got there?" said the Lion.

"Oh! I have got my mother's bones. She has been dead these forty- eleven years, and they say I must not keep her here, so I am taking her up into the middle of the mountains to bury her."

Then they parted. After he had gone a little way, the Lion said to himself, "I know that Anansi is a great rogue; I daresay he has got something there that he doesn't want me to see, and I will just follow him", but he took care not to let Anansi see him.

Now, when Anansi got into the wood he set his sacks down, and took one fish out and began to eat; then a fly came, and Anansi said, "I cannot eat any more, for there is someone near"; so he tied the sack up, and went on further into the mountains, where he set his sacks down, and took out two fish, which he ate. When no fly came, he said, "There's no one near"; so he took out more fish.

But when he had eaten about half-a-dozen, the Lion came up, and said, "Well, brother Anansi, a pretty tale you have told me."

"Oh! Brother Lion, I am so glad you have come; never mind what tale I have told you, but come and sit down. It was only my little bit of fun."

So Lion sat down and began to eat, but before Anansi had eaten two fish, Lion had emptied one of the sacks. Then Anansi said to himself, "'Greedy fellow, eating up all my fish."

"What do you say, sir?" asked the Lion.

"I only said you do not eat half fast enough", for Anansi was afraid the Lion would eat him up.

Then they went on eating, but Anansi wanted to revenge himself, and he said to the Lion, "Which of us do you think is the strongest?"

The Lion said, "Why, I am, of course."

Then Anansi said, "We will tie one another to the tree and we shall see which is the stronger."

Now they agreed that the Lion should tie Anansi first, and he tied him with some very fine string, and did not tie him tight. Anansi twisted himself about two or three times, and the string broke.

Then it was Anansi's turn to tie the Lion, and he took some very strong cord. The Lion said, "You must not tie me tight, for I did not tie you tight."

Anansi said, "Oh, no, to be sure I will not." But he tied him as tight as ever he could, and then told him to try and get loose.

The Lion tried and tried in vain. He could not get loose. Then Anansi thought, now is my chance; so he got a big stick and beat him, and then went away and left him, for he was afraid to untie him in case the Lion should kill him.

Now there was a woman called Miss Nancy, who was going out one morning to get some callalou (spinach) in the wood, and as she was going, she heard someone say, "Good morning, Miss Nancy!" She could not tell who spoke to her, but she looked where the voice came from, and saw the Lion tied to the tree.

"Good morning, Mr Lion, what are you doing there?"

He said, "It is that fellow Anansi who has tied me to the tree, but will you untie me?"

But she said, "No, for I am afraid, if I do, you will kill me."

But he gave, her his word he would not, but still she could not trust him, but he begged her again and again, and said:, "Well, if I do try to eat you, I hope all the trees will cry out shame upon me."

So at last she consented, but she had no sooner loosed him, than he came up to her to eat her, for he had been so many days without food that he was quite ravenous, but the trees immediately cried out "shame", and so he could not eat her. Then she went away as fast as she could, and the Lion found his way home.

When Lion got home he told his wife and children all that happened to him, and how Miss Nancy had saved his life, so they said they would have a great dinner, and ask Miss Nancy. Now when Anansi heard of it, he wanted to go to the dinner, so he went to Miss Nancy, and said she must take him with her as her child, but she said "No".

Then he said, I can turn myself into quite a little child, and then you can take me, and at last she said "Yes", and he told her, when she was asked what pap her baby ate, she must be sure to tell them it did not eat pap, but the same food as everyone else, and so they went, and had a very good dinner, and set off home again.

Somehow one of the lion's sons fancied that all was not right, and he told his father he was sure it was Anansi, and the Lion set out after him.

Now as they were going along, before the Lion got up to them, Anansi begged Miss Nancy to put him down, that he might run, which she did, and he got away and ran along the wood, and the Lion ran after him. When he found the Lion was overtaking him, he turned himself into an old man with a bundle of wood on his head, and when the Lion got up to him, he said, "Good-morning, Mr Lion", and the Lion said "Good-morning, old gentleman."

Then the old man said, "What are you after now?"

The Lion asked if he had seen Anansi pass that way, but the old man said "No, that fellow Anansi is always meddling with someone; what mischief has he been up to now?"

Then the Lion told him, but the old man said it was no use to follow him anymore, for he would never catch him, and so the Lion wished him good day, and turned and went home again.

THE FIGHTS OF MBUMA-TYETYE AND AN ORIGIN OF THE LEOPARD

This story has been edited and adapted from Robert Hamill Nassau's Where Animals Talk, first published in 1912 by Richard G. Badger at The Gorham Press, based out of Boston. This tale was originally told by storytellers from the Benga tribe.

Njambu built a Town. After he had finished the town, he married very many wives. After a short time they all bore children. There were many sons. He gave them names, and among them were Mbuma-tyetye and Njâ. After a short time Njambu's many wives became mothers again. This time, they gave birth to a large number of daughters. He gave them names as well.

Njambu's town was now full of men and women. They were crowded, and all busy. Some cut saplings, while others made rattan-ropes or went to cut the rattan-vine. Some shaped the bamboo for building and others made thatch. Everyone was busy

The town was full of noise. The villagers rejoiced in the abundance of people and Njambu and his sons gladly took dowries for their sisters, and gave them in marriage to young men from other towns. All in all, arguments were discussed and there were many stories told about White Men. There was much amusement amongst the people and much food was eaten, and the sons of Njambu married wives.

One day one of Njambu's sons, Mbuma-tyetye, said to his mother, "Make me some mekima, please, some mashed plantain."

His mother asked him, "Where are you going with the mekima?"

He answered, "I'm going to find someone to marry."

In the morning, he took his rolls of mashed plantains, and started out on his journey. He said to his mother, "You must look after my house."

He set off and on the road he met with two Rats, who were fighting. He took an ukima-roll, divided it, and gave it to them, saying, "Take this and eat."

They accepted, and told him, "You shall arrive at the end."

He went on, walking quickly, and met two Snakes fighting. He parted them. He took an ukima-roll and gave it to them.

They ate and they said to him, "You shall reach the end."

He went on with his journey, until ahead were two Millepedes fighting. He said to them, "Why are you trying to kill each other?"

He parted them, and gave them an ukima-roll.

They took it and said, "You shall reach the end!"

He lay down in the forest that night. At midnight, his mother saw something in her sleep that said, "Go with your two daughters in the morning, and take food for Mbuma-tyetye."

Early the next morning, she awoke her two daughters, and said, "Come! Let us go to follow after your brother, for he is still on his way."

They started out and went on until they found him sitting down by the path. They brought out the food from their traveling-bag, and they said, "We have come to give you food." They prepared the meal, and they ate. And they all slept that night in the forest.

Next morning, they started again, and they carried on with their journey. As they went on their way, they listened ahead, and they heard something, saying, "Eh! Fellows… Eh! Eh! Fellows… Eh! Nobody shall pass! Nobody shall pass here!"

When they drew near, they met an immense quantity of red stinging ants spread from the ground up to the tree-tops, entirely closing the way. Mbuma-tyetye and his company said, "Ah! These are the folk who were shouting here!" He advanced to fight the ants, and called to his younger sister, "Come on!"

She lifted her foot to tread upon the ants, and they instantly covered her from head to foot. He and his company tried in vain to draw her back, but the ants shouted, to strengthen themselves. "Eh! Fellows, eh!"

Mbuma-tyetye, still fighting, called to the elder sister, "Come on!"

Just as she lifted her foot, all of the red ants tried to cover her up too. The woman jumped to one side vigorously and stood there trying to calm herself down. Then she returned again to the ants, and they met in. battle once again.

She called out, "Ngalo! Hot water!" and it appeared. She took it, and threw it at the red ants, but they all went into their holes, and came out at another opening, again closing the path. She still stood there ready to fight, but they covered her, and dragged her off behind them. The ants shouted over their victory, "Eh! Fellows, eh! Today no person passes here!"

The son called to his mother, "Mother! Come on!"

His mother said, "My child, I am unable."

He called out, "Ngalo! Fire!"

Fire at once appeared. Mbuma-tyetye drew back the corpses of his sisters, seized the fire, and thrust it into the ants' nests. He also thrust it among the trees. The flames ignited them, and the surrounding forest burned to ashes, and the ants were all burned too. Then he brought his sisters to life, by taking the ashes, and throwing it over them, and down their throats into their stomachs.

When the day finally darkened, he said, "Ngalo! A house!"

A tent appeared at once with a table and tumblers and water and food. They sat there and ate. When they finished eating they talked about their experiences. When they ended, they said, "Let us lie down together." So they lay down for the night.

As dawn broke on the next day, a Partridge cried out, "Rise! Tyâtyâ lâ! Tyâtyâ lâ!" They washed their faces, set tea on the table, and drank it. They folded the tent-house, and swallowed it as a way of carrying it. They started on their journey, and talked all along the way.

As they went along, they heard something. They listened and heard a song. "Gribâmbâ! Eh! Gribâmbâ! Eh!"

Mbuma-tyetye and his mother and sisters kept on going toward the sound, which continued, "Dingâlâ! Eh! A person will not pass! No doubt about it! Dingâlâ! Eh! Wherever he comes from, he can pass here only by coming from above."

Mbuma-tyetye and his family approached the source of the song, and exclaimed, "There it is!" They went on and found the entire tribe of snails filling the road.

Mbuma-tyetye said to his mother, "What shall we do with the Kâ tribe?" They sat down to consider. They decided, "A fight! This very day!"

They sat and rested for a while. Then Mbuma-tyetye went ahead and shouted to his younger sister, "Come!"

She called out, "Ngalo! A short sword!" It appeared. She called again, "A strong cloth!" It appeared, and she dressed herself with it.

As she approached the snails, one of them fell on her head with a thud! She took the sword, and struck the snail. The snails shouted, "We're near you!" A crowd of them came on rapidly, one after another; in a heap, until they entirely covered her and she died! The snails swarmed over her, and pushing her behind them, they shouted in victory, "Tâkâ! Dingâlâ! Eh!"

Then the elder sister said she was going to help her brother in facing the snails. Her mother objected, "You? Stay here!"

But she replied, "Let me go!" She girded her body tightly, and then she entered the fight. The snails surrounded her. They were about to drag her to their rear, when she, at the side of the path, attempted to spring from them. But they swarmed over her and soon she too lay dead on the ground.

The mother was crying out, "Oh! My child!", when the snails covered her too.

Mbuma-tyetye retreated to rest for a short time, and called out, "Ngalo! A helmet!" It appeared. He fitted it to his head. He called again, "Ngalo! A glass of strong drink, and of water too!" It appeared. He asked for tobacco. It appeared. "Matches!" They appeared. He struck a match, and smoked. As he thrust the cigar in his mouth, it stimulated him and it told him things of the future in its clouds of smoke. After he had rested, he stood up, again for the fight.

The snails tuned their song:

"Iyâ! Dingâlâ! disabete!

Iyâ! Dingâlâ! sâlâlâsâlâ! Disabete!

Iyâ! Dingâlâ! Iyâ! Dingâlâ!

Iyâ! Dingâlâ! Sâlâlâsâlâ!

Iyâ! Dingâlâ! Eh! Bamo-eh!"

The snails, in their fierce charge, killed him, and were about to take away Mbuma-tyetye's corpse when, his Ngalo returned him to life. Mbuma-tyetye sprang up and cried out, "Ah! My Father Njambu! Dibadi-O!"

And he too took up his war-song:

"Tata Njambu ya milole, milole mi we.

Ta' Njambu! milole mi we.

Ta' Njambu! milole mi we.

Milole mi we. Ta' Njambu!"

All that while, the mother and his sisters were lying dead and the snails were shouting about their victory, "Tâkâ!"

Mbuma-tyetye took a short broad knife in his hands, and shouted, "Dibadi!" He girded his body firmly, and stood erect. He called out in challenge, "I've come!"

The snails answered, "You've reached the end!"

They fought. The man took his sword and the snails fell down upon him, but the man stood up, and moved forward. He laid hold of a small tree. He cut it, and whirled it around at the snails, and the snails fell down on the ground. But they rose up again flinging themselves upon the man.

The man jumped aside crying out, "Ah! My father Njambu! Dibadi-O!"

He took fire, thrust it among the tribe of snails, and every one fell down on the ground. Then he shaped a leaf into a funnel, and dropped a medicine into the noses of his mother and sisters. They slowly rose and tried to sit up. He poured the ashes of the snails over them, and they breathed it into their stomachs, and they came fully to life.

Then they said, "You are safe! Now, for our return home!"

He said, "Good! I wish you three safely home." And Mbuma-tyetye 's mother and sisters returned to their home.

Mbuma-tyetye continued his own journey until at a cross-roads, he found a giant Tooth, as large as a man. Tooth asked, "Where are you going?"

Said he, "I'm going to seek a marriage at a town owned by Njambu-ya-Mekuku."

Then, with his axe in hand, he turned aside from the path and chopped firewood. Then he kindly carried a lot of it and presented it to Tooth. He also opened his bag, and taking out an ukima roll, laid it down at the feet of Tooth with a bundle of gourd-seeds. Then he said, "I'm going."

But the giant Tooth, pleased with him, said to him, "Just wait!"

So, he waited, and, while waiting, Mbuma-tyetye said, "Ngalo! A fine house!" It appeared there. "A table!" There! "Good food!" There! "Fine drink!" There! Then the two of them ate, and drank, and had conversation together.

Tooth said to him, "Where you go, do not fear." It brought out from its hut a water-gourd, and said, "I will not show you more, nor will I tell you anything at all, but this Hova itself will tell you." Then Tooth said to him, "Go well!"

The man took the Gourd and kept it as close to him as if it was a great treasure. He started again on his journey, and had gone but a little way, when he found Kuda-nuts in immense abundance. He took up one, drew his knife, cracked the nut, and threw the kernel into his mouth. He stooped again, and was about to pick up another, when the Gourd warned him, "Stop! Stop!" So, he left the nuts.

He went on with his journey and found in abundance wild mangoes. He took one, split it, and bit out a piece, and was about to add another, when the warning came, "Stop! Stop!" So, he left the mangoes there, and yet his belly felt full. While still on his journey a great thirst for water seized him at a stream. He took his cup, plunged it into the water, filled it, drank, and was about to take more, when the warning came again, "Stop! Stop!" And he left the water. Yet his belly felt full.

Later on during his journey Mbuma-tyetye came to a large river. There he stood and listened and he heard a boat-song, "Ayehe, âhe! âyehe! E!" The sound of paddles passed by but he saw no person, nor did he see any canoe.

Gourd said to him, "Call them!"

Then he called out, "Who are you? Bring me a canoe!"

A voice replied, "Who are you?"

He answered, "I!"

The canoe came nearer, its crew singing, until it grounded on the beach. He saw what seemed to be just a great log!

Gourd said to him, "Embark!"

He got in. Instead of going straight across the river, they pulled far up stream, and then came all the way down again on the other side. As the paddlers came along, they constantly kept up the song, until they grounded at the landing-place at that other side of the river. Still he saw nothing of the invisible boatmen, when he landed.

As he climbed the stream bank, he saw a strange new town. He entered its public reception-house, and sat down. As he was looking for someone to come and speak with him, a Horn came and sat on his lap, and then moved away. A Bundle of Medicine came, sat, and moved away. A Bowl came and sat. A Spear came and sat. All these things saluted him. They were the People of that Town in disguise, but he saw none of them in their real form.

Gourd said to him, "Come and escort me into the back-yard."

He at once stepped out, and, when in the back-yard, it said. "Put me down.", for it had been carried suspended from his shoulder.

He put it down, standing it at the foot of a plantain-stalk. Gourd made a leaf funnel and dropped something into his eyes. His eyes suddenly opened, and he saw everything, and all the people, and the whole street.

Returning to the reception-house, he sat down again. Maidens came, who shone with such goodness as you have scarcely known! They were beautiful. The Chief of the town said, "Make food!" It was made at once. Then Mbuma-tyetye chose his wife.

Mbuma-tyetye and his wife were left sitting in the house. The wife began to weep, saying to herself, "What will his manner of eating be?"

The Gourd called him with a voice like the stroke of a bell. He went out to the Gourd, and it said to him, "When you eat, take one piece of plantain, one piece of flesh of the fowl, and then one spoonful of the wild-mango gravy. Put them in your mouth, and you shall say to her, 'You may remove the food.' Then you shall see what will happen."

He did all of this. His wife laughed in her heart, and she went and told her mother, "He is a person of sense."

The towns-people said to her, "What did he do?"

She evasively said to them. "Let us see!"

Later that evening, Mbuma-tyetye's new father-in-law said to him, "You have found us here in the midst of garden-making for your mother-in-law."

Mbuma-tyetye said. "That's good, Father!"

Gourd called to him, and told him, "It is not a garden. It is an entire forest, but it is not planted. It is all wild country. But, tomorrow, at daylight, early, you say to your wife that she must go and show you. You must take one young plantain-set, and a machete, and an axe. When you arrive there, then you shall say to her, 'Go back!' And she will go back. Then, you will slash with the machete and leave it. You must also take the axe and cut, and say, 'Ngunga-O! Mekud' O! Makako ma dibake man-jeya-O!' You shall see what will happen. Then you must insert the plantain-set in the ground. Finally you must set up a bellows, and work it. And you shall see what will happen."

The Gourd also knew but did not tell Mbuma-tyetye, that the Garden-Plan was made by the townspeople in order that he might weary of the task, which would mean that they could find an excuse for killing him, for they were Cannibals.

At daybreak, he did as he had been instructed. He called his wife. They went on until they came to the chosen spot. Said he, "Go back!" The woman went back. He did just as he had been directed, as to the clearing, and the felling, the incantation, and the planting. The plantains bore, and ripened at once. Every kind of food developed in that very hour. The man went back to the town, and sat down. They set some food before him.

The townsfolk then sent a child to spy out the garden. The child returned, excitedly saying, "Men! The entire forest is full with every type of food and everything is ripe."

The townsfolk said, "You're telling a lie! Let another child go and see."

Another boy went and returned with a ripe plantain held in his hand. In the evening, the Chief said to Mbuma-tyetye, "Sir, tomorrow people will have been filled with hunger for meat. A little pond belonging to your mother-in-law is over there. Tomorrow it is to be bailed out to get the fish that will be left in the bottom pools."

Gourd called to him. He went to it, and it said, "That is not a pond, it is a great river. However, when you go, you must take one log up stream and one log downstream. You shall see what will happen. Then you must bail only once, and say, 'Itata-O!' You shall see."

Next morning, he did as he had been told. The whole river was drained, and the fish were left in the middle. He returned to the town, and sat down. The people went to see, and, they were frightened at the abundance of fish. For a whole month, fish were gathered and fish still were left.

The Chief went to call his townspeople, saying, "We will do nothing to this fellow. Let him alone, for you have tried him with every test."

The townsfolk said, "Yes, and he has lingered here," Then they said, "Tomorrow there will be wrestling."

In the evening, the father-in-law called him, saying, "Mbuma-tyetye, tomorrow there is only wrestling. You have stayed long here. As you are about to go away with my child, there is only one thing more that she wants to see, and that is the wrestling tomorrow."

Gourd called him, and said to him, "It is not only for wrestling. You know the part of the village where the Wrestling-Ground lies. There is a big pit there. You will take care if you are near that pit, and you must push your opponents in."

In the evening, food was made, and soon it was ready. He and his wife ate, and finished. They engaged in conversation. They took pleasure over their love that night.

The next day, in the morning, very early, the drums began promptly. The Gourd called him, and handed him a leaf of magic-medicine, to hold in his hand, saying, "Go. Fear not!"

The townspeople began to shout a song back and forth to arouse enthusiasm. Two companies ranged on each side of the street, singing:

"Engolongolo! Hâ! Hâ!

Engolongolo! Hâ! Hâ!"

Engolongolo! Hâ! Hâ!

Engolongolo! Hâ! Hâ!"

Hearing their song as a challenge, Mbuma-tyetye went out of the house into the street. The strongest wrestler of the town, named Ekwamekwa, was missing, for he was out in the forest, felling trees.

When the towns-people saw Mbuma-tyetye standing in the street, they advanced all at once. He laid his hands upon them, and they all went back. He also stood back. Soon he advanced again, and a single opponent advanced. They laid their hands on each other's shoulders. The townspeople began another song, as if in derision:

"O! O! A!

O! O! A!

O! O! A!"

At once, Mbuma-tyetye seized his opponent, and threw him into the pit. Thereupon, his father-in-law shouted in commendation, "Iwâ!"

Another one came forward. Mbuma-tyetye advanced and as they met together, he took him, and threw him into the pit. Again his father-in-law shouted, "Iwâ!"

The sisters of the two men in the pit began to cry. The others said to the girls, "What are you doing? He shall die today! It is we who shall eat his entrails today!"

Another opponent came forward, and, as they met together, again the crowd sang out their derision:

"O! O! O! A!

O! O! O! A!

O! O! O! A!"

But, with one fling, Mbuma-tyetye cast him into the pit. "Iwâ" was repeated.

The sister of the last man to be thrown into the pit began to cry. The people rebuked her, "Mbâbâ! Mbâbâ! Join in the singing!"

Another man came forward. Mbuma-tyetye advanced again and as they came together, he lifted him, holding him by the foot. The singers, to encourage their man, said responsively, "Dikubwe! Dikubwe! Fear not an elephant with his tusks! Take off! Take off!"

Mbuma-tyetye lifted him, and promptly pushed him down into the pit with a thud.

The people began to call out anxiously, "We-e! We-e! O! They are overcome! They are overcome! Oh! Someone must go quickly and call Ekwamekwa, and tell him that people are being destroyed in the town, and he must come quickly."

Someone got up, and ran to call Ekwamekwa, wailing as he went, "Iyâ! Iyâ! Iyâ! Ekwamekwa, iyâ. Oh! Come! People are exterminated in the town!"

Ekwamekwa heard the cry. He snatched up his machete and axe, saying, "What is it?"

The messenger repeated, "Come! A being from above has destroyed many people in the town!"

Ekwamekwa, full of boasting, said, "Is it possible there are no men but me in the town?" He came, bristling with muscle, shouting, "Pwâ! Pwâ".

The drums were being beaten incessantly. The singers were shouting and the wrestlers' perspired freely. The noise of the people, of the drums, and sticks beating time were rattling, "Kwa, kwa, kwa!"

As Ekwamekwa appeared, the women and children raised their shrill voices. The shouters yelled, "A! Lâ! Lâ! Lâ! Lâ!"

Mbuma-tyetye advanced at once. He and Ekwamekwa laid hold of one another, and alternately pressed each other backward and forward. The one tried tricks to trip the other, and the other tried the same. Ekwamekwa held Mbuma-tyetye, and was about to throw him on the ground. Mbuma-tyetye jumped to one side, and stood there, his muscles quivering tensely. Ekwamekwa seized him about the waist and loins.

The people all were saying, "Let no one shout!" They said, "Make no noise! He is soon going to be eaten!" And it was a woman who said, "Get the cooking kettle ready!"

Ekwamekwa still held Mbuma-tyetye by the loins. So, they called out, "Down with him! Down with him!"

But Mbuma-tyetye shouted, "I'm here!" He put his foot behind Ekwamekwa's leg, and lifted him, and threw him into the pit.

Then there was a shout of distress by the people, "A, â, â, â!"

Ekwamekwa called out, "Catch him! Catch him!"

Mbuma-tyetye ran to his father-in-law's end of the town, and all the men came after him. His father-in-law protected him, and said to them, "You can do nothing with this stranger!"

At night, the Chief said to him, "Sir, you may go away tomorrow."

At daybreak, food was cooked. The Chief, Njambu-ya-Mekuku, put his daughters into large chests. In one was a lame daughter, in another was a daughter covered with skin disease, and another contained a daughter with a crooked nose, and others, with other defects were put into other chests. But the Chief put Mbuma-tyetye's wife into a poor chest all dirty outside with bird droppings all over it, and with smears of human excrement and ashes on it. In it he also placed a servant and all kinds of fine clothing. Then he said to Mbuma-tyetye, "Choose which chest contains your wife."

The Gourd at once called him, and it said to him, "Lift me up!" it whispered to him, "The chest which is covered with dirt and filth is the one which contains your wife. Even if they say, 'Ha, ha! He has had all his trouble for nothing;! He has left his wife,' nevertheless take it, and go on with your journey."

Mbuma-tyetye came to the spot where the chests were. The Chief said again, "Choose, from the chests, the one which contains your wife." Mbuma-tyetye picked up the poor one. The people shouted. But he at once started on his journey, and he went on until he came to the river. He stepped into a canoe, paddled to the other side, landed, and went on, carrying the chest. His magic Ngalo immediately transported Mbuma-tyetye to the home of the Great Tooth.

The Great Tooth asked, "How is it there?"

Mbuma-tyetye replied, "Good!"

The Gourd then said to its mother, the Tooth, "A fine fellow, that person there!"

Mbuma-tyetye went on with his journey, his feet treading firmly. Almost with one stride, in the twinkling of eyes, he was near the spring at his own town. Then he said, "Now let me open the chest here!"

On his opening it, a maiden attended by her servant came stepping out, arrayed in the clothing which had been placed in the chest for her. One's eyes would ache at sight of her silks, and the fine form of her person. And you or any other could say, "Yes! You are a bride! Truly a bride!"

Two young women rose up in the town to go to the spring to dip up water. They were just about to reach the spring, when they saw their brother and his wife and her servant. They went back together to the town, saying, "Well, if there isn't the woman whom Mbuma-tyetye has married! There are two women and himself!"

The town emptied to go and meet them on the path. His father took powder and guns, with which to announce the arrival, and cannon were roaring. When the young woman came and stood there in the street, there was shouting and shouting in admiration.

Another brother, named Njâ, when he came to see her, was so impressed with her that, without waiting for the salutations to be made, he said to his mother, "My mother! Make for me my mekima, too."

Mbuma-tyetye entered into the house with his wife. At once hot water was set before them, and they went to bathe. When they had finished, they entered the public reception-room. Njâ, impatient to get away and, in impolite haste, said, "Now, for my journey!"

Mbuma-tyetye advised him, "First wait. Let me tell you how the way is."

His brother replied, "No!" And he started off on his journey.

The others sat down to tell, and to hear the news. They told Mbuma-tyetye about the affairs of the town, and he told them how he had come back home. When he had completely finished, he was welcomed, "Iye! Oka! Oka-O! But now, sit down and stay."

Now, when Njâ had gone, he met the two Millepedes fighting. He exclaimed, "By my father Njambu! what is this?" He stood there laughing, "Kye! Kye! Kye!" He clapped his hands, "Kwâ! Kwâ! You there! Let me pass!"

They asked, "Give us an ukima."

He stood laughing, saying, "What will I see today! Food that is eaten by a human being! Is it so that they have teeth? As I see it, they, having no mouths, how can they eat?" But he opened his food-bag, took an ukima, and gave them a small piece.

They rebuked him for his meanness, and laid a curse on him, "Aye! You will not reach the end."

He responded, "I won't reach my end, eh? Humph! I'm going on my journey!" He left them, and they grabbed at the very little piece of ukima he had given them.

He cried out, "Journey!" and went on both by day and by night, traveling until he met the two Snakes fighting. He derided them, and took a club, and was about to strike them, when they cursed him, saying, "You will not reach the end!"

However, he gave them, at their request, an ukima, and passed on. As he turned to go, and was leaving them, they made signs behind him, repeating their curse, "He will not reach safety!" And they added, "He has no good sense. Let us leave him."

He still cried out, "Journey!" and went on to that place of Ihonga-na-Ihonga whose size filled all the width of the way. He made a shout, raising it very loud, and repeated his exclamation, "By my father, Njambu! You who have begotten me, you have not seen such as this!"

The Great Tooth asked, "Where are you going?"

He, astonished, exclaimed, "Ah! It can talk! Alas for me!" And he added a shout again, with laughter, "Kwati! Kwati! Kwati!"

The Great Tooth spoke and said, "Please, split for me fire-wood."

Njâ replied, "What will fire-wood do for you?" He, however, split the wood hastily, and left it in a pile.

It said, "Leave me an ukima."

Njâ responded, "Yes. Let me see what it will do with it now!" He opened his food-bag, and laid an ukima down disrespectfully, and said, "Eat! Let me see!"

Tooth said to him, "Sleep here!"

Said he, "If I sleep here, what is there for me to sit on?"

Tooth replied only, "Sleep here!"

Njâ said, "Yes!" Then he invoked his Ngalo, "A seat!" It appeared, and he sat down. In the evening, he invoked, "Ngalo, a house!" It appeared. "A bed!" It appeared. "A table!" It appeared. "Food!" It was set out. He ate, but did not offer any to Tooth, and fell into a deep sleep.

At daybreak, he was given water to wash his face, and food, and he ate it. Then Tooth said to him, "Now, this is a Hova. Go. The Hova will tell you what you should do."

Njâ said sarcastically "Good! A good thing!"

And he started on his journey. But, when he was gone, he despised the Gourd, and said to himself, "What can this water-jar do for me? I shall leave it here." And he laid it down at the foot of a Buda tree.

There were many kuda nuts lying on the ground. He prepared a seat, and sat down. He gathered the kuda nuts in one place. He took up a nut, broke it, threw its kernel into his mouth, and chewed it. He picked up another one, and was going to break it. Gourd warningly said, "I! I!"

Njâ replied, "Is it that you want me to give it to you?"

Gourd answered only, "I, I!"

And Njâ said, "But, then, your 'I! I!' what is it for?"

He broke many of the nuts, taking them up quickly, and soon finished eating all of them. And still his stomach felt empty, as if he had eaten nothing.

He then said, "The Journey!" He started, still carrying with him the Gourd, going on and on until he came to the Bwibe tree (wild mango). That Bwibe was sweet. He collected the mibe fruits, and began to split them. He split many in a pile, and then said, "Now! Let me suck!" He sucked them all, but he felt no sense of repletion, although the Gourd had warned him. He took the skins of the mibe fruit, and angrily thrust them inside the Gourd's mouth, saying, "Eat! You who have no teeth, what makes you say I must not eat? But, take these!"

He went on with his journey. And he found water. He took his drinking-vessel, plunged it into the water, dipped, put it to his mouth, drank, and drained the vessel. He wanted more, He plunged the vessel, and drank, draining the vessel once more. He took more again, disregarding the warnings of Gourd.

The water said to him, "Here am I, I remain myself. I will not satisfy you."

He gave up drinking, and started his journey again. He crossed some small creeks, and passed clear on, until he came to the river. As he listened, he heard songs passing by. He said to himself. "Now! Those who sing, where are they?"

The Gourd spoke to him, saying, "Call for the canoe!"

He replied, "How shall I call for a canoe, while I see no people?"

Gourd repeated to him, "Call!"

Then he shouted out, "You, bring me the canoe!"

Voices asked, "Who are you?"

He answered, "I am Njâ!"

Some of the voices said, "Come! Let us ferry him across."

Others said, "No!"

But the rest answered, "Come on!" Then they entered their canoe, laid hold of their paddles, and came singing:

"Kapi, madi, madi, sa!

Kapi, mada, mada, sa!"

And they came to the landing. Njâ saw nothing but what seemed to be a log, and he exclaimed, "How shall I embark in a log, while there is neither paddle, nor a person for a crew?"

But Gourd directed him, "Embark!"

So, he went in the log. They paddled, and brought him to the other side. He jumped ashore, and stood for a moment. Then he went on with the journey, walking on to a nearby town He saw nobody, but entered into the public reception-house, and sat down.

Gourd spoke to him, saying, "Come, and escort me to the back-yard."

He curtly answered, "Yes." He carried it, and stood it at the foot of a plantain stalk. Then he went back to the reception-house and sat down.

A bundle of medicines came to salute him, and was about to sit on his lap. He jumped up saying, "What is this?" He sat down again. Another bundle fell on his lap. He exclaimed, "Humph! What is that?"

The bundle being displeased, replied, "You will not come to the end."

The Gourd called him, and he went to the back-yard. The Gourd said to him, "Stand up!" And he stood up. Then the Gourd took a leaf, folded it as a funnel, and dropped a medicine into his eyes, and he began to see everything clearly.

He said, "This is the only thing which I can see that this Hova has done for me." He passed by, and entered the reception-house again, and sat down.

A person came saluting him, "Mbolo!"

He responded, "Ai!"

Another came, "Mbolo!"

He replied, "Ai!"

They cooked food, and got it ready to bring to him. While he was waiting he told the townsfolk about his errand, and he was given a wife.

Gourd called him. He went out to it and it directed him, "When you are going to eat, you must take only one piece of plantain, and a piece of the flesh of the fowl. Then you dip it into the udika-gravy, and put it into your mouth, and you will chew it, and when you have swallowed it, then you must leave the remainder of the food."

He said, "Yes! Yes!" And he laughed, "I do not know what this Hova means! And that 'remainder,' well, should I give it to the Gourd?" And he entered the house again, and sat down.

The food was set out. Little children came, and they said to each other, "Let us see how he will eat."

He took up a piece of plantain and put it in his mouth. He took a fowl's leg and put it in his mouth. He gnawed the flesh off of the bone. He took up another piece of plantain, dipped a spoon into the udika-gravy, and put it into his mouth. He took a piece of meat and a plantain, and swallowed them. The little children began to jeer at him, "He eats like a person who has never eaten before." He rose, but felt as if his stomach was empty.

He again seated himself, and he and his wife played games together. Soon he said, "My body feels exhausted with hunger". Food was again made and was set out and he ate. The result was the same. The evening meal was also prepared. He ate, and finished, and still was hungry.

In the evening, the Chief of the town called the tribe together and said to them, "Men! I see that this fellow has no sense. Let him return to his place."

The next day, Njâ said to himself, "Let me try and do what the Hova has advised me to do with the food."

The townsfolk cooked. They set food on the table. Njâ took a piece of plantain, and some flesh of the fowl. He placed them on a spoon, and dipped them into the udika, and put them into his mouth. He rose up, saying, "I have finished!" And his stomach felt replete. Then he thought to himself, "So! Is it possible that this Hova knows the affairs of the Spirits?"

The next time when food was spread on the table, he did the same thing and his stomach was satisfied.

Another day broke, and his father-in-law said to him, "On the morrow you will start your journey." When the next day dawned, the Chief brought out the chests containing his daughters, and said, "Now, then! Choose the one that you will take with you."

The Gourd whispered to him, "Do not take the fine-looking one. You must take the one you see covered with filth."

Njâ responded, "Not I!" The one he chose was the fine one. He took it up, and carried it away.

The town's-people began to cry out in pretence, "Oh! He has taken from us that fine maiden of ours!"

He was full of gladness that he was married. But, really, he was carrying a crooked-nosed woman whose body was nothing but skin-disease, with pus oozing all over her.

He went on his journey until he reached the town of the Great Tooth. crooked-nosed said, "Here's your Hova!"

The Tooth asked, "Tell me the news from there."

The Gourd whispered to Tooth, "Let this worthless fellow be! Let him go! He did not marry a real woman. So, he is not a person."

The man at once went on with his journey until he came to the spring by his own town. Njâ said, "Let me bathe!" He put down the chest, and plunged into the water. He bathed himself thoroughly, and emerged on the bank. Then he said to himself, "Now, then, let me open the chest!"

The key clicked, and the chest opened. A sick woman stepped out! He demanded, "Who brought you here?"

She replied, "You."

Said he in astonishment, "I?"

"Yes," she answered.

He, in anger, said, "Go back! Do not come at all to the town!" He at once started to go to the town and the woman slowly followed.

There were two children who were going to the spring. As they went, they met her and they cried out in fear, "Aye! Aye! Aye! A Ghost! Aye!" And they hurried back together to the town.

The town's-people asked them, "What's the matter?"

They said, "Come! There's a Ghost at the spring!"

The woman continued walking slowly.

Other children said, "Let us go! Does a Ghost come in the daytime? That is not so!"

As they ran along the path, they met her. They asked her, "Who has married you?"

She replied, "Isn't it Njâ?"

The children excitedly cried out shrilly, "A! Lâ! Lâ!" They went back quickly to the town, saying, "Come on! See the wife of Njâ!" The town emptied to go and see her. And they inquired of her, "Who is it who has married you?"

She answered, "Is it not Njâ?"

And the shrill cry of surprise rose again, "A! Lâ! Lâ! Lâ!"

When they reached the town, Njâ rose in anger from his house, picked up his spear, stood facing them, and threatened them with his spear, "This is it!"

He passed by the townsfolk and went into the back-yard. Once there he changed his body to that of a new kind of beast, with spots all over his skin. At once he stooped low on four legs, and thrust out his claws, and he began a fight with the people of the town. He was a Leopard. Then he went, leaping off into the Forest.

From then on he kept the name "Njâ," and has continued his fight with Mankind. The hatred between leopards and mankind dates from that time. Some of the people of that country had said to Mbuma-Tyetye that he would not be able to marry at the town of the Spirits, and had tried to hinder him. But he did go, and succeeded in marrying a daughter of Njambu-ya-Mekuku, while Njâ, attempting to do the same, and not waiting for advice from his brother, and treating the Spirits with disrespect on the way, failed.

THE COCK WHO CAUSED A FIGHT BETWEEN TWO TOWNS

This story has been edited and adapted from Elphinstone Dayrell's Folk Stories From Southern Nigeria, first published in 1910 by Longmans, Green And Company, London And New York.

Ekpo and Etim were half-brothers, that is to say they had the same mother, but different fathers. Their mother first of all had married a chief of Duke Town, when Ekpo was born, but after a time she got tired of him and went to Old Town, where she married Ejuqua and gave birth to Etim.

Both of the boys grew up and became very rich. Ekpo had a cock, of which he was very fond, and every day when Ekpo sat down to meals the cock used to fly on to the table and feed also. Ama Ukwa, a native of Old Town, who was rather poor, was jealous of the two brothers, and made up his mind if possible to bring about a quarrel between them, although he pretended to be friends with both.

One day Ekpo, the elder brother, gave a big dinner, to which Etim and many other people were invited. Ama Ukwa was also present. A very good dinner was laid for the guests, and plenty of palm wine was provided. When they had commenced to feed, the pet cock flew on to the table and began to feed off Etim's plate. Etim then told one of his servants to seize the cock and tie him up in the house until after the feast. So the servant carried the cock to Etim's house and tied him up for safety.

After much eating and drinking, Etim returned home late at night with his friend Ama Ukwa, and just before they went to bed, Ama Ukwa saw Ekpo's cock tied up. So early in the morning he went to Ekpo's house, who received him gladly.

About eight o'clock, when it was time for Ekpo to have his early morning meal, he noticed that his pet cock was missing. When he remarked upon its absence, Ama Ukwa told him that his brother had seized the cock the previous evening during the dinner, and was going to kill it, just to see what Ekpo would do. When Ekpo heard this, he was very vexed, and sent Ama Ukwa back to his brother to ask him to return the cock immediately. Instead of delivering the message as he had been instructed, Ama Ukwa told Etim that his elder brother was so angry with him for taking away his friend, the cock, that he would fight him, and had sent Ama Ukwa on purpose to declare war between the two towns.

Etim then told Ama Ukwa to return to Ekpo, and say he would be prepared for anything his brother could do. Ama Ukwa then advised Ekpo to call all his people in from their farms, as Etim would attack him, and on his return he advised Etim to do the same. He then arranged a day for the fight to take place between the two brothers and their people. Etim then marched his men to the other side of the creek, and waited for his brother; so Ama Ukwa went to Ekpo and told him that Etim had got all his people together and was waiting to fight. Ekpo then led his men against his brother, and there was a big battle, many men being killed on both sides. The fighting went on all day, until at last, towards evening, the other chiefs of Calabar met and determined to stop it; so they called the Egbo men together and sent them out with their drums, and eventually the fight stopped.

Three days later a big palaver was held, when each of the brothers was told to state his case. When they had done so, it was found that Ama Ukwa had caused the quarrel, and the chiefs ordered that he should be killed. His father, who was a rich man, offered to give the Egbos five thousand rods, five cows, and seven slaves to redeem his son, but they decided to refuse his offer.

The next day, after being severely flogged, he was left for twenty-four hours tied up to a tree, and the following day his head was cut off.

Ekpo was then ordered to kill his pet cock, so that it should not cause any further trouble between himself and his brother, and a law was passed that for the future no one should keep a pet cock or any other tame animal.

THE ELECTION OF THE KING BIRD

This story has been edited and adapted from Elphinstone Dayrell's Folk Stories From Southern Nigeria, first published in 1910 by Longmans, Green And Company, London And New York.

Old Town, Calabar, once had a king called Essiya, who, like most of the Calabar kings in the olden days, was rich and powerful, but although he was so wealthy, he did not possess many slaves. He therefore used to call upon the animals and birds to help his people with their work. In order to get the work done quickly and well, he determined to appoint head chiefs of all the different species. The elephant he appointed king of the beasts of the forest, and the hippopotamus king of the water animals, until at last it came to the turn of the birds to have their king elected.

Essiya thought for some time which would be the best way to make a good choice, but could not make up his mind, as there were so many different birds who all considered they had claims. There was the hawk with his swift flight, and of hawks there were several species. There were the herons to be considered, and the big spur-winged geese, the hornbill or toucan tribe, and the game birds, such as guinea-fowl, the partridge, and the bustards. Then again, of course, there were all the big crane tribe, who walked about the sandbanks in the dry season, but who disappeared when the river rose, and the big black-and-white fishing eagles. When the king thought of the plover tribe, the sea-birds, including the pelicans, the doves, and the numerous shy birds who live in the forest, all of whom sent in claims, he got so confused, that he decided to have a trial by ordeal of combat, and sent word round the whole country for all the birds to meet the next day and fight it out between themselves, and that the winner should be known as the king bird ever afterwards.

The following morning many thousands of birds came, and there was much screeching and flapping of wings. The hawk tribe soon drove all the small birds away, and harassed the big waders so much, that they very shortly disappeared, followed by the geese, who made much noise, and winged away in a straight line, as if they were playing "Follow my leader." The big forest birds who liked to lead a secluded life very soon got tired of all the noise and bustle, and after a few croaks and other weird noises went home. The game birds had no chance and hid in the bush, so that very soon the only birds left were the hawks and the big black-and-white fishing eagle, who was perched on a tree calmly watching everything. The scavenger hawks were too gorged and lazy to take much interest in the proceedings, and were quietly ignored by the fighting tribe, who were very busy circling and swooping on one another, with much whistling going on. Higher and higher they went, until they disappeared out of sight. Then a few would return to earth, some of them badly torn and with many feathers missing.

At last the fishing eagle said, "When you have quite finished with this foolishness please tell me, and if any of you fancy yourselves at all, come to me, and I will settle your chances of being elected head chief once and for all."

When they saw his terrible beak and cruel claws, knowing his great strength and ferocity, the hawks stopped fighting between themselves, and acknowledged the fishing eagle to be their master.

Essiya then declared that Ituen, which was the name of the fishing eagle, was the head chief of all the birds, and should thenceforward be known as the king bird.

From that time to the present day, whenever the young men of the country go to fight they always wear three of the long black-and-white feathers of the king bird in their hair, one on each side and one in the middle, as they are believed to impart much courage and skill to the wearer, and if a young man is not possessed of any of these feathers when he goes out to fight, he is looked upon as a very small boy indeed.

DOG AND HIS FALSE FRIEND LEOPARD

This story has been edited and adapted from Robert Hamill Nassau's Where Animals Talk, first published in 1912 by Richard G. Badger at The Gorham Press, based out of Boston. This tale was originally told by storytellers from the Benga tribe.

Dog and Leopard built a town. Dog then begot very many children. Leopard begot his many also. They had one table together. They conversed, they hunted, they ate, they drank.

One day, they were arguing. Leopard said, "If I hide myself, you are not able to see me."

Dog replied, "There is no place in which you can hide where I cannot see you."

The next day, at the break of the day, Leopard emerged from his house at Batanga, and he went north as far as from there to Bahabane near Plantation. Dog, in the next morning, emerged. He asked, "Where is chum Njâ?"

The women and children answered, "We do not know."

Dog also started, and went, and as he went, smelling the scent of Leopard, he soon arrived at Plantation. He came and stood under the tree up which Leopard was hidden and he said, "Is not this you?"

Both of them returned, and came to their town. Food had been prepared, and they ate. Leopard said, "Chum, you will not see me here tomorrow." When the next day began to break, Leopard started southward, as far as to Lolabe. Next day, in the morning, Dog stood out in the street, lifted up his nose, and smelled. He also went down southward, clear on till he came to Lolabe, and standing at the foot of a tree, he said, "Is not this you?"

Leopard came down from the top of the tree. They stood and then they returned to their town. Food was cooked for them; they ate, and finished.

Leopard said, "Chum, you will not see me tomorrow again, no matter what may take place."

Dog asked, "True?"

Leopard replied, "Yes!"

In the morning, Leopard started southward, for a distance like from Batanga to Campo River, which is about 40 miles.

At the opening of the next day, Dog emerged, and, standing and smelling, he said, looking toward the south, "He went this way." Dog also went to Campo. He reached Leopard, and said, "Is not this you?"

They came back to their town, where they were made food, and they ate.

The next day, Leopard emerged early. He went northward, as far as from Batanga to Lokonje, again about 40 miles. Dog sniffed the air, and followed north also. In a steady race, he was soon there, and he reached Leopard. So, Leopard said, "It is useless, I will not attempt to hide myself again from Mbwa."

Thereupon, Dog spoke to Leopard and said, "It is I, whom, if I hide myself from you, you will not see."

Leopard replied, "What? Even if you were able to find me, how much more should I be able to find you!"

So, Dog said to him, "Wait, till daybreak."

When the next day broke, Dog passed from his house like a flash unseen, to Leopard's house. Dog lay down underneath Leopard's bed in his public Reception-house.. Then Leopard, who had not seen him, came to the house of Dog. He asked the women, "Where is Mbwa?"

They said, "Your friend, long ago, has gone out, very early."

Leopard returned to his house, and he said to his children, "That fellow! If I catch him I do not know what I shall do to him!"

He started southward on his journey, as far as Lolabe, and did not see Dog. So he returned northward a few miles, as far as Boje, and did not see him. Down again south to Campo, and he did not see him. That first day, he did not find him at all. Then he returned toward Batanga, and went eastward to Nkâmakâk, which is about 60 miles, and he did not see him. He went on northward to Ebaluwa, but again he did not see him. He went north-west to Lokonje but he did not see him. And Leopard, wearied, went back to his town.

Coming to the bed, not knowing Dog was still there, he lay down very tired. He said to his people, "If I had met him today, then you would be eating a good meat now." All these words were said while Dog was underneath the bed.

Then Dog leaped out. Leopard asked, "Where have you been?"

Dog answered, "I saw you when you first passed out."

Leopard said, "True?"

And Dog says, "Yes!"

Then Dog went out to his end of the town. And, knowing that Leopard intended evil toward him, he said to his children, "Let us go and dig a pit." So they went and dug a pit in the middle of the road.

Then Dog told his wives and children, "Go away from here at once!" He also said, "I and this little Mbwa, which can run so fast, we shall remain behind." Then the others went on in advance.

Dog warned this young one, "When you are pursued, you must jump clear across that pit."

Then Dog, to cover the retreat of his family, came alone to Leopard's end of the town. He and his children chased after him. Dog ran away rapidly, and escaped.

When Leopard's company arrived at the house of Dog, they found there only that little dog. So they said, "Come on, for there is no other choice than that we catch and eat this little thing."

Thereupon, Leopard chased after the little dog, but it leaped away rapidly, and Leopard ran after him. When the little Dog was near the pit, it made a jump. When Leopard came to the pit, he fell inside, tumbling!

Dog's other enemy Gorilla was following after Leopard. He also fell into the pit, headlong! Finding Leopard there, Gorilla said, "What is this?"

Leopard stood at one side, and Gorilla at the other. They paced around and around each other snarling and cursing.

Dog, standing at the edge above, was laughing at them, saying, "Fight your own fight! Wasn't it me that you wanted? "

But Leopard and Gorilla were not fighting in the pit. If the one approached, the other retreated.

Dog spoke to them and said in derision. "I am just a weakling, but I have outwitted both of you!"

THE KING'S MAGIC DRUM

This story has been edited and adapted from Elphinstone Dayrell's Folk Stories From Southern Nigeria, first published in 1910 by Longmans, Green And Company, London And New York.

Efriam Duke was an ancient king of Calabar. He was a peaceful man, and did not like war. He had a wonderful drum, the property of which, when it was beaten, was always to provide plenty of good food and drink. So whenever any country declared war against him, he used to call all his enemies together and beat his drum; then to the surprise of every one, instead of fighting the people found tables spread with all sorts of dishes, such as fish, foo-foo, palm-oil chop, soup, cooked yams and ocros, and plenty of palm wine for everybody. In this way he kept all the country quiet, and sent his enemies away with full stomachs, and in a happy and contented frame of mind.

There was only one drawback to possessing the drum, and that was, if the owner of the drum walked over any stick on the road or stepped over a fallen tree, all the food would immediately go bad, and three hundred Egbo men would appear with sticks and whips and beat the owner of the drum and all the invited guests very severely.

Efriam Duke was a rich man. He had many farms and hundreds of slaves, a large store of kernels on the beach, and many puncheons of palm-oil. He also had fifty wives and many children. The wives were all fine women and healthy; they were also good mothers, and all of them had plenty of children, which was good for the king's house.

Every few months the king used to issue invitations to all his subjects to come to a big feast, and even the wild animals were invited; the elephants, hippopotami, leopards, bush cows, and antelopes used to come, for in those days there was no trouble, as they were friendly with man, and when they were at the feast they did not kill one another. All the people and the animals as well were envious of the king's drum and wanted to possess it, but the king would not part with it.

One morning Ikwor Edem, one of the king's wives, took her little daughter down to the spring to wash her, as she was covered with yaws, which are bad sores all over the body. The tortoise happened to be up a palm tree, just over the spring, cutting nuts for his midday meal, and while he was cutting, one of the nuts fell to the ground, just in front of the child. The little girl, seeing the good food, cried for it, and the mother, not knowing any better, picked up the palm nut and gave it to her daughter. Directly the tortoise saw this he climbed down the tree, and asked the woman where his palm nut was. She replied that she had given it to her child to eat. Then the tortoise, who very much wanted the king's drum, thought he would make plenty palaver over this and force the king to give him the drum, so he said to the mother of the child, "I am a poor man, and I climbed the tree to get food for myself and my family. Then you took my palm nut and gave it to your child. I shall tell the whole matter to the king, and see what he has to say when he hears that one of his wives has stolen my food," for this, as everyone knows, is a very serious crime according to native custom.

Ikwor Edem then said to the tortoise, "I saw your palm nut lying on the ground, and thinking it had fallen from the tree, I gave it to my little girl to eat, but I did not steal it. My husband the king is a rich man, and if you have any complaint to make against me or my child, I will take you before him."

So when she had finished washing her daughter at the spring she took the tortoise to her husband, and told him what had taken place. The king then asked the tortoise what he would accept as compensation for the loss of his palm nut, and offered him money, cloth, kernels or palm-oil, all of which things the tortoise refused one after the other.

The king then said to the tortoise, "What will you take? You may have anything you like."

And the tortoise immediately pointed to the king's drum, and said that it was the only thing he wanted.

In order to get rid of the tortoise the king said, "Very well, take the drum," but he never told the tortoise about the bad things that would happen to him if he stepped over a fallen tree, or walked over a stick on the road.

The tortoise was very glad at this, and carried the drum home in triumph to his wife, and said, "I am now a rich man, and shall do no more work. Whenever I want food, all I have to do is to beat this drum, and food will immediately be brought to me, and plenty to drink."

His wife and children were very pleased when they heard this, and asked the tortoise to get food at once, as they were all hungry. This the tortoise was only too pleased to do, as he wished to show off his newly acquired wealth, and was also rather hungry himself, so he beat the drum in the same way as he had seen the king do when he wanted something to eat, and immediately plenty of food appeared, so they all sat down and made a great feast.

The tortoise did this for three days, and everything went well; all his children got fat, and had as much as they could possibly eat. He was therefore very proud of his drum, and in order to display his riches he sent invitations to the king and all the people and animals to come to a feast. When the people received their invitations they laughed, as they knew the tortoise was very poor, so very few attended the feast, but the king, knowing about the drum, came, and when the tortoise beat the drum, the food was brought as usual in great profusion, and all the people sat down and enjoyed their meal very much.

They were much astonished that the poor tortoise should be able to entertain so many people, and told all their friends what fine dishes had been placed before them, and that they had never had a better dinner. The people who had not gone were very sorry when they heard this, as a good feast, at somebody else's expense, is not provided every day. After the feast all the people looked upon the tortoise as one of the richest men in the kingdom, and he was very much respected in consequence. No one, except the king, could understand how the poor tortoise could suddenly entertain so lavishly, but they all made up their minds that if the tortoise ever gave another feast, they would not refuse again.

When the tortoise had been in possession of the drum for a few weeks he became lazy and did no work, but went about the country boasting of his riches, and took to drinking too much. One day after he had been drinking a lot of palm wine at a distant farm, he started home carrying his drum, but having had too much to drink, he did not notice a stick in the path. He walked over the stick, and of course the Ju-Ju was broken at once. But he did not know this, as nothing happened at the time, and eventually he arrived at his house very tired, and still not very well from having drunk too much. He threw the drum into a corner and went to sleep. When he woke up in the morning the tortoise began to feel hungry, and as his wife and children were calling out for food, he beat the drum, but instead of food being brought, the house was filled with Egbo men, who beat the tortoise, his wife and children, badly. At this the tortoise was very angry, and said to himself, "I asked everyone to a feast, but only a few came, and they had plenty to eat and drink. Now, when I want food for myself and my family, the Egbos come and beat me. Well, I will let the other people share the same fate, as I do not see why I and my family should be beaten when I have given a feast to all people."

He therefore at once sent out invitations to all the men and animals to come to a big dinner the next day at three o'clock in the afternoon.

When the time arrived many people came, as they did not wish to lose the chance of a free meal a second time. Even the sick men, the lame, and the blind got their friends to lead them to the feast. When they had all arrived, with the exception of the king and his wives, who sent excuses, the tortoise beat his drum as usual, and then quickly hid himself under a bench, where he could not be seen. His wife and children he had sent away before the feast, as he knew what would surely happen.

Directly he had beaten the drum three hundred Egbo men appeared with whips, and started flogging all the guests, who could not escape, as the doors had been fastened. The beating went on for two hours, and the people were so badly punished, that many of them had to be carried home on the backs of their friends. The leopard was the only one who escaped, as directly he saw the Egbo men arrive he knew that things were likely to be unpleasant, so he gave a big spring and jumped right out of the compound.

When the tortoise was satisfied with the beating the people had received he crept to the door and opened it. The people then ran away, and when the tortoise gave a certain tap on the drum all the Egbo men vanished. The people who had been beaten were so angry, and made so much palaver with the tortoise, that he made up his mind to return the drum to the king the next day. So in the morning the tortoise went to the king and brought the drum with him. He told the king that he was not satisfied with the drum, and wished to exchange it for something else; he did not mind so much what the king gave him so long as he got full value for the drum, and he was quite willing to accept a certain number of slaves, or a few farms, or their equivalent in cloth or rods.

The king, however, refused to do this, but as he was rather sorry for the tortoise, he said he would present him with a magic foo-foo tree, which would provide the tortoise and his family with food, provided he kept a certain condition. This the tortoise gladly consented to do. Now this foo-foo tree only bore fruit once a year, but every day it dropped foo-foo and soup on the ground. And the condition was, that the owner should gather sufficient food for the day, once, and not return again for more.

The tortoise, when he had thanked the king for his generosity, went home to his wife and told her to bring her calabashes to the tree. She did so, and they gathered plenty of foo-foo and soup quite sufficient for the whole family for that day, and went back to their house very happy.

That night they all feasted and enjoyed themselves. But one of the sons, who was very greedy, thought to himself, "I wonder where my father gets all this good food from? I must ask him."

So in the morning he said to his father, "Tell me where do you get all this foo-foo and soup from?"

But his father refused to tell him, as his wife, who was a cunning woman, said "If we let our children know the secret of the foo-foo tree, some day when they are hungry, after we have got our daily supply, one of them may go to the tree and gather more, which will break the Ju-Ju."

But the envious son, being determined to get plenty of food for himself, decided to track his father to the place where he obtained the food. This was rather difficult to do, as the tortoise always went out alone, and took the greatest care to prevent any one following him. The boy, however, soon thought of a plan, and got a calabash with a long neck and a hole in the end. He filled the calabash with wood ashes, which he obtained from the fire, and then got a bag which his father always carried on his back when he went out to get food. In the bottom of the bag the boy then made a small hole, and inserted the calabash with the neck downwards, so that when his father walked to the foo-foo tree he would leave a small trail of wood ashes behind him.

Then when his father, having slung his bag over his back as usual, set out to get the daily supply of food, his greedy son followed the trail of the wood ashes, taking great care to hide himself and not to let his father perceive that he was being followed. At last the tortoise arrived at the tree, and placed his calabashes on the ground and collected the food for the day, the boy watching him from a distance. When his father had finished and went home the boy also returned, and having had a good meal, said nothing to his parents, but went to bed. The next morning he got some of his brothers, and after his father had finished getting the daily supply, they went to the tree and collected much foo-foo and soup, and so broke the Ju-Ju.

At daylight the tortoise went to the tree as usual, but he could not find it, as during the night the whole bush had grown up, and the foo-foo tree was hidden from sight. There was nothing to be seen but a dense mass of prickly tie-tie palm. Then the tortoise at once knew that someone had broken the Ju-Ju, and had gathered foo-foo from the tree twice in the same day; so he returned very sadly to his house, and told his wife. He then called all his family together and told them what had happened, and asked them who had done this evil thing. They all denied having had anything to do with the tree, so the tortoise in despair brought all his family to the place where the foo-foo tree had been, but which was now all prickly tie-tie palm, and said, "My dear wife and children, I have done all that I can for you, but you have broken my Ju-Ju. You must therefore for the future live on the tie-tie palm."

So they made their home underneath the prickly tree, and from that day you will always find tortoises living under the prickly tie-tie palm, as they have nowhere else to go to for food.

A PLEA FOR MERCY

This story has been edited and adapted from Robert Hamill Nassau's Where Animals Talk, first published in 1912 by Richard G. Badger at The Gorham Press, based out of Boston. This tale was originally told by storytellers from the Benga tribe.

These four Beasts were living in one town; Civet, in his own house; Tortoise in his; Antelope also in his; Genet too in his own. But their four houses opened on to one long street.

One day, in the afternoon, they all were in that street, sitting down in conversation. Tortoise said to them, "I have here a word to say."

They replied "Well! Speak!"

At that time, their town had a great famine. So, Tortoise said, "Tomorrow, we will go to seek food."

They replied, "Good! Just as soon as the day, at its first break."

Then they scattered, and went to their houses to lie down for sleep. Soon, the day broke. And they all got up, and were ready by sunrise at six o'clock.

They all went on their journey to find food. They searched as they walked a distance of several miles. Then they came to a plantation of Njambo's wife Ivenga. It was distant from Njambo's town about one hour's walk. It had a great deal of sugar-cane; also of yams and cassava. It had also a quantity of sweet potatoes. Njambo's chickens were also accustomed to go to scratch for worms among the plants.

At once, Civet exclaimed, "I'll go no further! I like to eat sugar-cane!" So he went to the plot of cane.

Antelope also said, "I too! I'll not go any further. I like to eat leaves of potato and cassava." So he went to the plot of cassava.

And Genet said, "Yes! I see Kuba here! I like to eat Kuba! I'll go no further!" So, he went after the chickens.

But first, the three had asked Tortoise, "Kudu! what will you do? Have you nothing to eat?"

Tortoise answered, "I have nothing to eat. But, I shall await you even two days, and will not complain."

So, Civet remarked, "Yes! I will not soon leave here, till I eat up all this cane. Then I will go back to town."

Antelope also said, "Yes, the same. I will remain here with the potato leaves till I finish them, before I go back."

Genet also said, "Yes! I see many Kuba here. I will stay and finish them."

Tortoise only said, "I have nothing to say."

In that plantation there was a large tree and Tortoise went to lie down at its foot.

They were all there about four days, eating and eating. On the fifth day, Njambo's wife Ivenga said to herself, "I'll go today, and see about my plantation, how it is."

She came to the plantation, and when she saw the condition in which it was, she lifted up her voice, and began to wail a lamentation. She saw that little cane was left, and not many potatoes. Looking in another part of the plantation, she saw lying there, very many chicken feathers.

She ran back rapidly to town to tell her husband. But, she was so excited she could scarcely speak. He asked her, "What's the matter, Ivenga?"

She answered, "I have no words to tell you. For, the Plantation is left with no food."

Then, the Man called twenty men of the town, and he said to them, "Take four nets!"

They took the nets, and also four dogs, with small bells tied to the necks of the dogs. The men had also guns and spears and machetes in their hands. They followed into the forest and they came on to three of the Beasts. They came first upon Antelope, with their dogs, and they shot him dead. Then the dogs came on Genet, and they followed him and soon he was shot with a gun. They came also on Civet, and killed him.

Taking up the carcasses, they said to each other, "Let us go back to town." On the way, they came to the big Tree, and found Tortoise lying at the base. They took him also, and then went on to their town.

When they arrived Njambo ordered, "Put Kudu in a house and suspend him from the roof." Also he ordered, "Take off the skin of Vyâdu and hang it in the house where Kudu is." He added, "Take off also the skin of Njâbu."

They did so, and they put it into that house. He directed that Genet should also be skinned, and his skin hung in that same house. So, there was left of these beasts in the street, only the flesh of their bodies. These the men cut up and divided among themselves. And they feasted for several days.

On the fourth day afterward, Njambo said to his wife, "I'm going on a visit to a town about three miles away. While I am away, kill Kudu, and prepare him with ngândâ for me, by my return."

The woman got ready the ngândâ seeds for the pudding, and then went into the room to take Tortoise. In the dim light, she lifted up her hand, and found the string that suspended Tortoise.

But, before she untied it, Tortoise said, "Just wait a little." The woman took away her hand, and stood waiting. Tortoise asked her, "This skin there looks like what?"

The woman replied, "A skin of Vyâdu."

And Tortoise inquired, "What did Vyâdu do?"

The woman answered, "Vyâdu ate my potatoes in the Plantation, and my husband killed him for it."

Tortoise said, "That is well." Then Tortoise again asked, "This other skin is of what animal?"

The woman replied, "Of Uhingi."

Tortoise inquired, "What did Uhingi do?"

The woman answered, "Uhingi killed and ate my and my husband's Kuba, and he was killed for that."

Then Tortoise said, "Very good reason!" Again Tortoise asked the woman, "This other skin?"

She answered, "Of Njâbu."

Tortoise asked, "Njâbu, what did he do?"

She answered, "Njâbu ate my sugar-cane, and my husband killed him."

Tortoise said, "A proper reason! But, you, you are going to kill me and cook me with ngândâ-pudding. What have I done?"

The woman had no reason to give. So she left Tortoise alive, and began to cook the gourd-seeds with fish.

Soon, Njambo himself came back, and his wife set before him the ngândâ and fish. But he objected, "Ah! my wife! I told you to cook Kudu, and you have cooked me fish. Why?"

The woman told him, "My husband! First finish this food, and then you and I will go to see about Kudu." So, Njambo finished eating, and Ivenga removed the plates from the table. Then they two went into the room where Tortoise was suspended.

The woman sat, but Njambo was standing ready to pluck down Tortoise. Then Tortoise said to Njambo, "You, Man! Just wait!"

The woman also said to Njambo, "My husband! listen to what Kudu says to you."

Tortoise asked, "You, Man, what skin is this?"

Njambo answered, "Of Vyâdu. I killed him on account of this eating my Plantation."

Then Tortoise asked, "And that skin?"

Njambo answered, "Of Uhingi, and I killed him for eating my Kuba."

Tortoise again asked, "And this other?"

Njambo answered, "Of Njâbu; for eating my sugar-cane."

Then Tortoise said, "There were four of us in the Plantation. What have I eaten? Tell me. If I have eaten, then I should die."

Njambo told him, "I've found no reason against you."

Tortoise then asked, "Then, why should I die?"

So, Njambo untied Tortoise from the roof, and said to Ivenga, "Let Kudu go, for, I find no reason against him. Let him go as he pleases."

So, Ivenga set Tortoise free and he hurried back to his town in peace.

THE MAN AND THE DOUKANA TREE

This story has been edited and adapted from the appendix of George Webbe Dasent's Popular Tales From The Norse, first published in 1907 by Edmonston and Douglas, based out of Edinburgh, Scotland.

There was once a man and his wife, who were very poor, and they had a great many children. The man was very lazy, and would do nothing to help his family. The poor mother did all she could. In the wood close by grew a Doukana Tree, which was full of fruit. Every day the man went and ate some of the fruit, but never took any home, so he ate and he ate, until there were only two Doukanas left on the Tree. One he ate, and left the other. Next day, when he went for that one, he was obliged to climb up the tree to reach it, but when he got up, the Doukana fell down; when he got down the Doukana jumped up, and so it went on until he was quite tired.

Then he asked all the animals that passed by to help him, but they all made some excuse. They all had something to do. The horse had his work to do, or he would have no grass to eat. The donkey brayed. Last came a dog, and the man begged him hard to help him, so the dog said he would. Then the man climbed up the tree, and the Doukana jumped to the ground again. The dog picked it up and ran off with it The man was very vexed, and ran after the dog, but it ran all the faster, so that the man could not overtake him. The dog, seeing the man after him, ran to the sea shore, and scratching a hole in the ground, buried every bit of himself except his nose, which he left sticking out.

Soon after the man came up, and seeing the nose, cried out that he had 'never seen ground with a nose', and catching hold of it he tugged till he pulled out the dog. He squeezed him with all his might to make him give up the Doukana. And that's why dogs are so small in their bodies to this very day.

THE WOMAN WITH TWO SKINS

This story has been edited and adapted from Elphinstone Dayrell's Folk Stories From Southern Nigeria, first published in 1910 by Longmans, Green And Company, London And New York.

Eyamba of Calabar was a very powerful king. He fought and conquered all the surrounding countries, killing all the old men and women, but the able-bodied men and girls he caught and brought back as slaves, and they worked on the farms until they died.

This king had two hundred wives, but none of them had borne a son to him. His subjects, seeing that he was becoming an old man, begged him to marry one of Anansi's daughters, as they always had plenty of children. But when the king saw Anansi's daughter he did not like her, as she was ugly, and the people said it was because her mother had had so many children at the same time. However, in order to please his people he married the ugly girl, and placed her among his other wives, but they all complained because she was so ugly, and said she could not live with them. The king, therefore, built her a separate house for herself, where she was given food and drink the same as the other wives. Every one jeered at her on account of her ugliness, but she was not really ugly, but beautiful, as she was born with two skins, and at her birth her mother was made to promise that she should never remove the ugly skin until a certain time during the night, and that she must put it on again before dawn.

Now the king's head wife knew this, and was very fearful lest the king should find it out and fall in love with Anansi's daughter; so she went to a Ju-Ju man and offered him two hundred rods to make a potion that would make the king forget altogether that Anansi's daughter was his wife. This the Ju-Ju man finally consented to do, after much haggling over the price. He charged three hundred and fifty rods and he made up some "medicine," which the head wife mixed with the king's food. For some months this had the effect of making the king forget Anansi's daughter, and he used to pass quite close to her without recognising her in any way.

When four months had elapsed and the king had not once sent for Adiaha, for that was the name of Anansi's daughter, she began to get tired, and went back to her parents. Her father, Anansi, then took her to another Ju-Ju man, who, by making spells and casting lots, very soon discovered that it was the king's head wife who had made the Ju-Ju and had enchanted the king so that he would not look at Adiaha. He therefore told Anansi that Adiaha should give the king some medicine which he would prepare, which would make the king remember her. He prepared the medicine, for which Anansi had to pay a large sum of money, and that very day Adiaha made a small dish of food, into which she had placed the medicine, and presented it to the king. Directly he had eaten the dish his eyes were opened and he recognised his wife, and told her to come to him that very evening. So in the afternoon, being very joyful, she went down to the river and washed, and when she returned she put on her best cloth and went to the king's palace.

Directly it was dark and all the lights were out she pulled off her ugly skin, and the king saw how beautiful she was, and was very pleased with her, but when the cock crowed Adiaha pulled on her ugly skin again, and went back to her own house.

This she did for four nights running, always taking the ugly skin off in the dark, and leaving before daylight in the morning. In course of time, to the great surprise of all the people, and particularly of the king's two hundred wives, she gave birth to a son, but what surprised them most of all was that only one son was born, whereas her mother had always had a great many children at a time, generally about fifty.

The king's head wife became more jealous than ever when Adiaha had a son, so she went again to the Ju-Ju man, and by giving him a large present induced him to give her some medicine which would make the king sick and forget his son. And the medicine would then make the king go to the Ju-Ju man, who would tell him that it was his son who had made him sick, as he wanted to reign instead of his father. The Ju-Ju man would also tell the king that if he wanted to recover he must throw his son away into the water.

And the king, when he had taken the medicine, went to the Ju-Ju man, who told him everything as had been arranged with the head wife. But at first the king did not want to destroy his son. Then his chief subjects begged him to throw his son away, and said that perhaps in a year's time he might get another son. So the king at last agreed, and threw his son into the river, at which the mother grieved and cried bitterly.

Then the head wife went again to the Ju-Ju man and got more medicine, which made the king forget Adiaha for three years, during which time she was in mourning for her son. She then returned to her father, and he got some more medicine from his Ju-Ju man, which Adiaha gave to the king. And the king knew her and called her to him again, and she lived with him as before. Now the Ju-Ju who had helped Adiaha's father, Anansi, was a Water Ju-Ju, and he was ready when the king threw his son into the water, and saved his life and took him home and kept him alive. And the boy grew up very strong.

After a time Adiaha gave birth to a daughter, and the jealous wife also persuaded the king to throw this little girl away as well. It took a longer time to persuade him, but at last he agreed, and threw his daughter into the water too, and forgot Adiaha again. But the Water Ju-Ju was ready again, and when he had saved the little girl, he thought the time had arrived to punish the action of the jealous wife, so he went about amongst the head young men and persuaded them to hold a wrestling match in the market-place every week. This was done, and the Water Ju-Ju told the king's son, who had become very strong, and was very like to his father in appearance, that he should go and wrestle, and that no one would be able to stand up before him. It was then arranged that there should be a grand wrestling match, to which all the strongest men in the country were invited, and the king promised to attend with his head wife.

On the day of the match the Water Ju-Ju told the king's son that he need not be in the least afraid, and that his Ju-Ju was so powerful, that even the strongest and best wrestlers in the country would not be able to stand up against him for even a few minutes. All the people of the country came to see the great contest, to the winner of which the king had promised to present prizes of cloth and money, and all the strongest men came. When they saw the king's son, whom nobody knew, they laughed and said, "Who is this small boy? He can have no chance against us." But when they came to wrestle, they very soon found that they were no match for him. The boy was very strong indeed, beautifully made and good to look upon, and all the people were surprised to see how closely he resembled the king.

After wrestling for the greater part of the day the king's son was declared the winner, having thrown everyone who had stood up against him. In fact, some of his opponents had been badly hurt, and had their arms or ribs broken owing to the tremendous strength of the boy. After the match was over the king presented him with cloth and money, and invited him to dine with him in the evening. The boy gladly accepted his father's invitation, and after he had had a good wash in the river, put on his cloth and went up to the palace, where he found the head chiefs of the country and some of the king's most favoured wives.

They then sat down to their meal, and the king had his own son, whom he did not know, sitting next to him. On the other side of the boy sat the jealous wife, who had been the cause of all the trouble. All through the dinner this woman did her best to make friends with the boy, with whom she had fallen violently in love on account of his beautiful appearance, his strength, and his being the best wrestler in the country. The woman thought to herself, "I will have this boy as my husband, as my husband is now an old man and will surely soon die." The boy, however, who was as wise as he was strong, was quite aware of everything the jealous woman had done, and although he pretended to be very flattered at the advances of the king's head wife, he did not respond very readily, and went home as soon as he could.

When he returned to the Water Ju-Ju's house he told him everything that had happened, and the Water Ju-Ju said, "As you are now in high favour with the king, you must go to him to-morrow and beg a favour from him. The favour you will ask is that all the country shall be called together, and that a certain case shall be tried, and that when the case is finished, the man or woman who is found to be in the wrong shall be killed by the Egbos before all the people."

So the following morning the boy went to the king, who readily granted his request, and at once sent all around the country appointing a day for all the people to come in and hear the case tried. Then the boy went back to the Water Ju-Ju, who told him to go to his mother and tell her who he was, and that when the day of the trial arrived, she was to take off her ugly skin and appear in all her beauty, for the time had come when she need no longer wear it. This the son did.

When the day of trial arrived, Adiaha sat in a corner of the square, and nobody recognised the beautiful stranger as Anansi's daughter. Her son then sat down next to her, and brought his sister with him. Immediately his mother saw her she said, "This must be my daughter, whom I have long mourned as dead," and embraced her most affectionately.

The king and his head wife then arrived and sat on their stones in the middle of the square, all the people saluting them with the usual greetings. The king then addressed the people, and said that he had called them together to hear a strong palaver at the request of the young man who had been the victor of the wrestling, and who had promised that if the case went against him he would offer up his life to the Egbo. The king also said that if, on the other hand, the case was decided in the boy's favour, then the other party would be killed, even though it were himself or one of his wives; whoever it was would have to take his or her place on the killing-stone and have their heads cut off by the Egbos. To this all the people agreed, and said they would like to hear what the young man had to say. The young man then walked round the square, and bowed to the king and the people, and asked the question, "Am I not worthy to be the son of any chief in the country?" And all the people answered "Yes!"

The boy then brought his sister out into the middle, leading her by the hand. She was a beautiful girl and well made. When everyone had looked at her he said, "Is not my sister worthy to be any chief's daughter?" And the people replied that she was worthy of being any one's daughter, even the king's. Then he called his mother Adiaha, and she came out, looking very beautiful with her best cloth and beads on, and all the people cheered, as they had never seen a finer woman. The boy then asked them, "Is this woman worthy of being the king's wife?" And a shout went up from every one present that she would be a proper wife for the king, and looked as if she would be the mother of plenty of fine healthy sons.

Then the boy pointed out the jealous woman who was sitting next to the king, and told the people his story, how that his mother, who had two skins, was Anansi's daughter. He told of how she had married the king, and how the head wife was jealous and had made a bad Ju-Ju for the king, which made him forget his wife. He spoke well of how she had persuaded the king to throw himself and his sister into the river, which, as they all knew, had been done, but the Water Ju-Ju had saved both of them, and had brought them up.

Then the boy said: "I leave the king and all of you people to judge my case. If I have done wrong, let me be killed on the stone by the Egbos. If, on the other hand, the woman has done evil, then let the Egbos deal with her as you may decide."

When the king knew that the wrestler was his son he was very glad, and told the Egbos to take the jealous woman away, and punish her in accordance with their laws. The Egbos decided that the woman was a witch, so they took her into the forest and tied her up to a stake, and gave her two hundred lashes with a whip made from hippopotamus hide, and then burnt her alive, so that she should not make any more trouble, and her ashes were thrown into the river. The king then embraced his wife and daughter, and told all the people that she, Adiaha, was his proper wife, and would be the queen for the future.

When the palaver was over, Adiaha was dressed in fine clothes and beads, and carried back in state to the palace by the king's servants.

That night the king gave a big feast to all his subjects, and told them how glad he was to get back his beautiful wife whom he had never known properly before, also his son who was stronger than all men, and his fine daughter. The feast continued for a hundred and sixty-six days, and the king made a law that if any woman was found out getting medicine against her husband, she should be killed at once. Then the king built three new compounds, and placed many slaves in them, both men and women. One compound he gave to his wife, another to his son, and the third he gave to his daughter. They all lived together quite happily for some years until the king died, when his son came to the throne and ruled in his stead.

"DEATH BEGINS BY SOME ONE PERSON": A PROVERB

This story has been edited and adapted from Robert Hamill Nassau's Where Animals Talk, first published in 1912 by Richard G. Badger at The Gorham Press, based out of Boston. This tale was originally told by storytellers from the Benga tribe.

Snail, Igwana and Tortoise all lived together in one village. One day, Tortoise went to roam in the forest. There he found a large tree called Evenga. He said to himself, "I will stay at the foot of this tree, and wait for the fruit to fall." For two days, he remained there alone.

On the third day, Igwana said to Snail, "I must go and search for our Chum Kudu, wherever he is."

So, Igwana went and he found Tortoise in a hole at the foot of that tree. Igwana said to him, "Chum! For two days I haven't seen you!"

Tortoise replied, "I shan't go back to the village; I will remain here."

Then Igwana said to him, "Well, then, let us sit here together in the same spot."

Tortoise objected, "No!"

So Igwana climbed up the trunk a very short distance, and clung there.

After two days, Snail, who had been left alone, said to himself, "I must follow my friends, and find where they are."

So, Snail journeyed, and found Tortoise and Igwana there at that tree. Looking at the tree, he exclaimed, "Ah! What a fine tree under which to sit!"

The others replied, "Yes, stay here!"

So Snail said to Igwana, "I will stay near you, Chum Ngâmbi, where you are."

But Igwana objected, "No!"

There was a vine hanging down from the treetop to the ground, and Snail climbed up the vine. Thus the three friends were arranged; Tortoise in the hole at the foot of the tree, Igwana up the trunk a short way, and Snail on the vine half-way to the top.

Igwana held on where he was, close to the bark of the tree. He was partly deaf, and did not hear well.

After two days, the tree put forth a great abundance of fruit. The fruit all ripened. Very many small Birds came to the tree-top to eat the fruit. And very many small Monkeys too, at the top. Also big monkeys. And also big birds. All crowded at the top. They all began to eat the fruit. As they ate, they played, and made a great deal of noise.

Tortoise hearing this noise, and dreading that it might attract the notice of some enemy, called to Igwana, "Ngâmbi! Tell Kâ to say to those people there at the top of the tree, to eat quietly, and not with so much noise."

Tortoise himself did not call to Snail, lest his shout should add to the noise. He only spoke in a low voice to Igwana. But, to confirm his words, he quoted a proverb, "Iwedo a yalakendi na moto umbaka", which means that death begins by one person. This meant that they all should be watchful, in case Danger come to them all by the indiscretion of a few. But Igwana did not hear, and was silent.

Tortoise called again, "Ngâmbi! Tell Kâ to tell those people to eat quietly, and without noise."

Igwana was silent, and made no answer. A third and a fourth time, Tortoise called out thus to Igwana, but he did not hear. So, Tortoise said to himself, "I won't say any more!"

A man from Njambo's Town had gone out to hunt, having with him bow and arrow, a machete, and a gun. In his wandering, he happened to come to that tree. Hearing the noise of voices, he looked up and saw the many monkeys and birds on the tree. He exclaimed to himself, "Ah! How very many on one tree, more than I have ever seen!"

He shot his arrow, and three monkeys fell. He fired his gun, and killed seven birds. Then the Birds and the Monkeys all scattered and fled in fear. The Man also looked at the foot of the tree, and saw Tortoise in the hole. He drew him out, and thrust him into his hunting-bag. Then he looked on the other side of the tree, and saw Igwana within reach. He rejoiced in his success, "Oh! Igwana here too!" He struck him with the machete, and Igwana died.

Observing the vine, the Man gave it a pull. And down fell Snail! The Man exclaimed, "So! This is Snail!"

As the Man started homeward carrying his load of animals, Tortoise in the bag, mourning over his fate, said to the dead Igwana and the others, "I told you to call to Kâ to warn Kema and Lonani, and, now death has come to us all! If you, Kema and Lonani, in the beginning, on the tree-top, had not made such a noise, Man would not have come to kill us. This all comes from you."

And Man took all these animals to his town, and divided them among his people.

WHY THE CAT KILLS RATS

This story has been edited and adapted from Elphinstone Dayrell's Folk Stories From Southern Nigeria, first published in 1910 by Longmans, Green And Company, London And New York.

Ansa was King of Calabar for fifty years. He had a very faithful cat as a housekeeper, and a rat was his house-boy. The king was an obstinate, headstrong man, but was very fond of the cat, who had been in his store for many years.

The rat, who was very poor, fell in love with one of the king's servant girls, but was unable to give her any presents, as he had no money.

At last he thought of the king's store, so in the night-time, being quite small, he had little difficulty, having made a hole in the roof, in getting into the store. He then stole corn and native pears, and presented them to his sweetheart.

At the end of the month, when the cat had to render her account of the things in the store to the king, it was found that a lot of corn and native pears were missing. The king was very angry at this, and asked the cat for an explanation. But the cat could not account for the loss, until one of her friends told her that the rat had been stealing the corn and giving it to the girl.

When the cat told the king, he called the girl before him and had her flogged. The rat he handed over to the cat to deal with, and dismissed them both from his service. The cat was so angry at this that she killed and ate the rat, and ever since that time whenever a cat sees a rat she kills and eats it.

WHY ANANSI RUNS WHEN HE IS ON THE SURFACE OF WATER

This story has been edited and adapted from Captain R. S. Rattray's Akan-Ashanti Folk-Tales, first published in 1930 by Oxford University Press – American Branch, New York.

One day, Kwaku Anansi went to Okraman the Dog and told him he wished to build a new village to live in. Okraman heard Anansi's suggestion and agreed with it, and Anansi then explained his plan.

Okraman was to collect a rope-creeper on the Monday following the next Sunday Adae. Anansi would do the same, and the two would then meet together. Anansi told Okraman that he would gather a gourd and fill it with water and wished the Dog to do so also so that the pair would have water in case their destination lacked it. Okraman agreed again and the two both prepared once the Sunday Adae began, and Anansi even put honey into his gourd for extra measure. Then, the two travelled the next Monday.

Okraman and Anansi had reached the half-way point on their journey when the two became exhausted, and the Dog recommended they both rest for a moment and drink some of the water they'd prepared. Then, Anansi suggested that they play a game to pass the time while they rested. Okraman asked the Spider which type of game he wished to play, and Anansi replied that he wished to play a binding game. Anansi then explained the rules of the game.

Okraman would tie Anansi, and then Anansi would tie Okraman. Anansi would give Okraman a signal, and the Dog would try to escape his bindings. Okraman however wanted Anansi to tie him first. Anansi disagreed, scolding the Dog, and reminded Okraman that he was his elder, causing Okraman to accept Anansi's terms in their game. Thus, the two began and Okraman tied Anansi first.

However, Anansi did not know that Okraman was also hungry and had no true desire to play Anansi's game. Instead, the Dog bound Anansi and carried him away, hoping to sell the Spider for food. Once Anansi realized Okraman's plan, he began mourning, but the Dog paid him no mind, continuing to carry Anansi away until they both reached a stream.

Soon, someone else noticed Anansi's cries and came to investigate them, and that was Odenkyem the Crocodile. He asked Okraman about the matter but the Dog was too frightened to respond. Instead, Okraman dropped Anansi and fled, while Odenkyem freed Anansi from his bindings. Anansi thanked the Crocodile and asked if there was a means he could repay him for his kindness, but Odenkyem said that he didn't want anything in return. Yet, Anansi was insistent and told Odenkyem that if he had children he would come and style them, dressing their hair so that they could be very beautiful. Odenkyem accepted this, and did not suspect Anansi's deception.

Anansi returned home after speaking to the Crocodile and told his wife Aso that he needed palm-nuts and onions for a stew he planned to make. He said that he would bring a crocodile back to supply meat for it. Aso did so, while Anansi gathered a knife, sharpening it. He mashed some eto, and carried it with him to the stream where Odenkyem lived. Next, Anansi called out to Odenkyem and told the Crocodile that he'd prepared a reward for him, sitting the eto in the water. Odenkyem heard Anansi and soon came, ready to accept Anansi's gift. However, the Spider had tricked him.

Anansi withdrew his knife and cut the Crocodile with it, but the blow he dealt to Odenkyem was not fatal. Anansi didn't realize this however, and left for home without a second thought. Aso noticed Anansi didn't have the crocodile he'd promised to bring home to prepare stew and asked him where it was, but Anansi became defensive, scolding his wife for bothering him when he'd just returned home. Aso however, saw through Anansi's attitude, and told her husband that she could tell he had not gotten Odenkyem like he'd planned. Anansi could only remain silent, and said nothing else about the matter for the remainder of the evening.

Morning began and Aso told Anansi she was going to the river. The Crocodile was still laying there when she arrived, and flies now surrounded him; Aso took note of this, and told Anansi what she'd observed when she returned to their home. Anansi explained to Aso that he'd used a special medicine to kill Odenkyem and thus had to wait until the next day before he collected his kill. He then thanked her for confirming the crocodile had died and set about for the stream on his own, with a stick he'd prepared for defence.

Anansi soon arrived and noticed Odenkyem was still laying in the riverbank. He carefully strode over to the Crocodile's body, poking him with his stick. Then, Anansi prodded Odenkyem's body and asked the Crocodile if he was dead, shifting his body over as he examined him, but Odenkyem did not respond. Little did Anansi know that the Crocodile may have been motionless, but he was far from deceased.

Anansi eventually stopped prodding the Crocodile with his stick, convinced he was dead, and edged closer to Odenkyem's body, stretching his hand out to check the Crocodile a final time. Yet, Anansi's action would prove to be a mistake, for he immediately found himself trapped between the Crocodile's jaws when he clasped the Spider unexpectedly. After a great contest between the two, Anansi wiggled himself free from Odenkyem and fled the river, rushing back home. So it is that Anansi always runs while crossing the water, careful to never give Odenkyem another chance to capture him again.

THE KING AND THE ANT'S TREE

This story has been edited and adapted from the appendix of George Webbe Dasent's Popular Tales From The Norse, first published in 1907 by Edmonston and Douglas, based out of Edinburgh, Scotland.

There was a King who had a very beautiful daughter, and he said, whoever would cut down an Ant's tree, which he had in his kingdom, without brushing off the ants, should marry his daughter. Now a great many came and tried, but no one could do it, for the ants fell out upon them and stung them, and they were forced to brush them off. There was always someone watching to see if they brushed the ants off.

Then Anansi went, and the King's son was set to watch him. When they showed him the tree, he said, "Why, that's nothing, I know I can do that."

So they gave him the axe, and he began to hew, but each blow he gave the tree, he shook himself and brushed himself, saying all the while, "Did you see me do that? I suppose you think I'm brushing myself, but I am not."

And so he went, on until he had cut down the tree. But the boy thought he was only pretending to brush himself all the time, and the King was obliged to give him his daughter.

"NUTS ARE EATEN BECAUSE OF ANGÂNGWE"; A PROVERB

This story has been edited and adapted from Robert Hamill Nassau's Where Animals Talk, first published in 1912 by Richard G. Badger at The Gorham Press, based out of Boston. This tale was originally told by storytellers from the Mpongwe tribe.

The Hogs had cleared a space in the forest, for the building of their town. They were many, numbering men and women and children.

In another place, a Hunter was sitting in his town. Every day, at daybreak, he went out to hunt. When he returned in the afternoons with his prey, he left it a short distance from the town, and entering his house, would say to his women and children, "Go to the outskirts of the town, and bring what animal you find I have left there."

One day, having gone hunting, he killed Elephant. The children went out to cut it up and bring it in. Another day, he killed Gorilla. And so, each day, he killed some animal. He never failed to obtain something.

One day, his children said to him, "You always return with some animal, but you never have brought us Ngowa."

He replied, "I saw many Ingowa today, when I was out there. But, I wonder at one thing;. When they are all together eating, and I approach, they run away. As to Ingowa, they eat nkula nuts and I know where the trees are. Well, then, I ambush them, but, when I go nearer, I see one big

Ngowa not eating, but going around and around the herd. Whether it sees me or does not see me, it is true that when I get ready to aim my gun, then they all scatter. The reason that Ingowa escape me, I do not know."

The Hogs, when they had finished eating, and were returning to their own town, as they passed the town of Elephant, heard the sounds of mourning. They asked, "Who is dead?"

The answer was, "Njâgu is dead! Njâgu is dead!"

They inquired, "He died of what disease?"

They were told, "Not disease. Hunter killed him."

Then another day, when Ox was killed and his people were heard mourning for him. Another day, Antelope was killed and his people were mourning for him. All these animals were dying because of Hunter killing them.

At first, the Hogs felt pity for all these other Beasts. But, when they saw how they were dying, they began to mock at them, "These are not people! They only die! But, as to us Ingowa, Hunter is not able to kill us. We hear only the report that there is such a person as Hunter, but he is not able to kill us."

When Hogs were thus boasting, their King, Angângwe, laughed at them, saying, "You don't know, you Ingowa! You mock others, because Hunter kills them?"

They answered, "Yes, we mock them, for, we go to the forest as they do, but Hunter does not touch us."

Angângwe asked, "When you go to the forest do you all eat your inkula-nuts using just your own strength and skill?"

They answered, "Yes. We go to the forest on our own feet. We pick up and eat the inkula. No one feeds us."

Angângwe said, "It is not so. Those inkula you eat are eaten because of a person."

They insisted, "No, it is not so. Inkula have no person in particular to do anything for them."

Thus they had this long discussion, the Hogs and their King, and they got tired of it, and lay down to sleep.

In the morning, when daylight came, the King said, "A journey for nuts! But, today, I am sick. I am not able to go to gather nuts with you. I will stay in town."

The Hogs said, "Well! We know the way. It is not necessary for you to go."

When they went, they were jeering about their King, "Angângwe said, 'Inkula si nyo o'kângâ w' oma', but we will see what we can do today without him."

They went to the nkula trees, and found great abundance fallen to the ground during the night. The herd of Hogs, when they saw all these inkula, jumped about in joy. They stooped down to pick up the nuts, their eyes busy with the ground. They ate and ate. None of them thought of Hunter, and whether he was out in the forest.

But, that very morning, Hunter had risen, taken his gun and ammunition-box, and had gone to hunt. And, after a while, he had seen the Hogs in the distance. They were only eating and eating, not looking at anything but nuts.

Hunter said in his heart, "These Hogs, I see them often, but why have I not been able to kill them?" He crept softly nearer and nearer. After creeping closer and closer he then stood up to spy. He did this many times but he did not see the big Hog which, on other days, he had always observed going around and around the herd. Hunter stooped close to the ground, and crept onward. Then, as he approached closer, the Hogs still went on eating. He bent his knee to the earth, and he aimed his gun! Ingowa were still eating! His gun flashed! Ten Hogs died!

The Hogs fled, some of them wounded. Those who were not wounded, stopped before they reached their town, and said, "Let us wait for the wounded." They waited. When the hindmost caught up and joined the others, they showed them their wounds, some in the head, some in the legs.

These wounded ones said, "As we came, we saw no others behind us. There are ten of us missing. We think they are dead." So, they all returned toward their Town, and, on their way, began to mourn.

When they had come clear on to the town, Angângwe asked, "What news do you bring me?"

They answered, "Angângwe! Evil news! But we do not know what is the matter. We only know that the words you said are not really so, that 'nuts are eaten because of a certain person.' Because, when we went, each one of us gathered by his own skill, and ate by his own strength, and no one trusted to anyone else. And when we went, we ate abundantly, and everything was good. Except that, Hunter has killed ten of us. And many others are wounded."

The King inquired, "Well! Have you brought nuts for me who was left in Town?"

They replied, "No. When Hunter shot us, we feared, and could no longer wait."

Then Angângwe said, "I told you that inkula are eaten because of a person, and you said, 'not so.' And you still doubt me."

Another day, the Hogs went for inkula and the King remained in town. And, as on the other day, Hunter killed them. So, for five successive days the King stayed in town while the Hogs went into the forest, where Hunter killed them.

Finally, Angângwe said to himself, "Ingowa have become great fools. They do not admit that nuts are eaten by reason of a certain person. They see how Hunter kills them, but they still doubt my words. I pity them.

Tomorrow, I will go with them to the nuts. I will explain to them how Hunter kills them."

So, in the morning, the King ordered, "Come all to nuts! But when we go for the nuts, if I say, 'Ngh-o-o!' then every one of you who are eating them must start to town, and not come back, because then I have seen or smelt Hunter, and I grunt to let you know."

All the Hogs agreed. They went on clear to the nkula trees, and ate, stooping with eyes to the ground. But Angângwe, not eating, kept looking here and there. He sniffed wind from south to north, and assured them, "Eat! I am here!" He watched and watched, and presently he saw a speck far away. He passed around to sniff the wind. His nose uplifted, he caught the odour of Hunter. He returned to the herd and grunted "Ngh-o-o", and they all fled. They arrived safely at town.

Then he asked them, "Who is dead? Who is wounded?"

They assured him, "None."

He said, "Good!"

Thus they went nutting, for five consecutive days, and their King, Angângwe kept watch. And none of them died by Hunter.

Then Angângwe said to them, "Today let us have a conversation." And he began, "I told you, inkula si nyo o'kângâ w' oma. You said, 'Not so!' But, when you went by yourselves to eat nuts, did not Hunter kill you? And these last five days when we have gone together and you obeyed my voice, then who has died?"

They then replied, "No one! No one! Indeed, you spoke truly. You are justified. Inkula si nyo o'kângâ wa 'Ngângwe. It is so!"

WHY THE WORMS LIVE UNDERNEATH THE GROUND

This story has been edited and adapted from Elphinstone Dayrell's Folk Stories From Southern Nigeria, first published in 1910 by Longmans, Green And Company, London And New York.

When Eyo was ruling over all men and animals, he had a very big palaver house to which he used to invite his subjects at intervals to feast. After the feast had been held and plenty of tombo had been drunk, it was the custom of the people to make speeches. One day after the feast the head driver ant got up and said he and his people were stronger than any one, and that no one, not even the elephant, could stand before him, which was quite true. He was particularly offensive in his allusions to the worms, whom he disliked very much, and said they were poor wriggling things.

The worms were very angry and complained, so the king said that the best way to decide the question of who was the stronger was for both sides to meet on the road and fight the matter out between themselves to a finish. He appointed the third day from the feast for the contest, and all the people turned out to witness the battle.

The driver ants left their nest in the early morning in thousands and millions, and, as is their custom, marched in a line about one inch broad densely packed, so that it was like a dark-brown band moving over the country. In front of the advancing column they had out their scouts, advance guard, and flankers, and the main body followed in their millions close behind.

When they came to the battlefield the moving band spread out, and as the thousands upon thousands of ants rolled up, the whole piece of ground was a moving mass of ants and bunches of struggling worms. The fight was over in a very few minutes, as the worms were bitten in pieces by the sharp pincer-like mouths of the driver ants. The few worms who survived squirmed away and buried themselves out of sight.

King Eyo decided that the driver ants were easy winners, and ever since the worms have always been afraid and have lived underground, and if they happen to come to the surface after the rain they hide themselves under the ground whenever anything approaches, as they fear all people.

THE WOMAN, THE APE, AND THE CHILD

This story has been edited and adapted from Elphinstone Dayrell's Folk Stories From Southern Nigeria, first published in 1910 by Longmans, Green And Company, London And New York.

Okun Archibong was one of King Archibong's slaves, and lived on a farm near Calabar. He was a hunter, and used to kill bush buck and other kinds of antelopes and many monkeys. The skins he used to dry in the sun, and when they were properly cured, he used to sell them in the market. The monkey skins were used for making drums, and the antelope skins were used for sitting mats. The flesh, after it had been well smoked over a wood fire, he also sold, but he did not make much money.

Okun Archibong married a slave woman called Nkoyo, who had previously worked for King Duke. He paid a small dowry, took his wife home to his farm, and in the dry season time she had a son. About four months after the birth of the child Nkoyo worked on the farm while her husband was absent hunting. She placed the little boy under a shady tree and went about her work, which was clearing the ground for the yams which would be planted about two months before the rains.

Every day while the mother was working a big ape used to come from the forest and play with the little boy. He used to hold him in his arms and carry him up a tree, and when Nkoyo had finished her work, he used to bring the baby back to her. There was a hunter named Edem Effiong who had for a long time been in love with Nkoyo, and had made advances to her, but she would have nothing to do with him, as she was very fond of her husband.

When she had her little child Effiong Edem was very jealous, and meeting her one day on the farm without her baby, he said, "Where is your baby?"

And she replied that a big ape had taken it up a tree and was looking after it for her. When Effiong Edem saw that the ape was a big one, he made up his mind to tell Nkoyo's husband. The very next day he told Okun Archibong that he had seen his wife in the forest with a big ape. At first Okun would not believe this, but the hunter told him to come with him and he could see it with his own eyes. Okun Archibong therefore made up his mind to kill the ape.

The next day he went with the other hunter to the farm and saw the ape up a tree playing with his son, so he took very careful aim and shot the ape, but it was not quite killed. It was so angry, and its strength was so great, that it tore the child limb from limb and threw it to the ground. This so enraged Okun Archibong that seeing his wife standing near he shot her also. He then ran home and told King Archibong what had taken place.

This king was very brave and fond of fighting, so as he knew that King Duke would be certain to make war upon him, he immediately called in all his fighting men. When he was quite prepared he sent a messenger to tell King Duke what had happened. Duke was very angry, and sent the messenger back to King Archibong to say that he must send the hunter to him, so that he could kill him in any way he pleased. This Archibong refused to do, and said he would rather fight.

Duke then got his men together, and both sides met and fought in the market square. Thirty of Duke's men were killed, and twenty were killed on Archibong's side, and there were also many wounded. On the whole King Archibong had the best of the fighting, and drove King Duke back. Finally, when the fighting was at its hottest, the other chiefs sent out all the Egbo men with drums and stopped the fight, and the next day the palaver was tried in Egbo house. King Archibong was found guilty, and was ordered to pay six thousand rods to King Duke.

He refused to pay this amount to Duke, and said he would rather go on fighting, but he did not mind paying the six thousand rods to the town, as the Egbos had decided the case. They were about to commence fighting again when the whole country rose up and said they would not have any more fighting, as Archibong said to Duke that the woman's death was not really the fault of his slave Okun Archibong, but of Effiong Edem, who made the false report.

When Duke heard this he agreed to leave the whole matter to the chiefs to decide, and Effiong Edem was called to take his place on the stone. He was tried and found guilty, and two Egbos came out armed with cutting whips and gave him two hundred lashes on his bare back, and then cut off his head and sent it to Duke, who placed it before his Ju-Ju.

From that time to the present all apes and monkeys have been frightened of human beings, and even of little children. The Egbos also passed a law that a chief should not allow one of his men slaves to marry a woman slave of another house, as it would probably lead to fighting.

THE STORY OF THE LEOPARD, THE TORTOISE, AND THE BUSH RAT

This story has been edited and adapted from Elphinstone Dayrell's Folk Stories From Southern Nigeria, first published in 1910 by Longmans, Green And Company, London And New York.

At the time of the great famine all the animals were very thin and weak from want of food, but there was one exception, and that was the tortoise and all his family, who were quite fat, and did not seem to suffer at all. Even the leopard was very thin, in spite of the arrangement he had made with the animals to bring him their old grandmothers and mothers for food.

In the early days of the famine the leopard had killed the mother of the tortoise, in consequence of which the tortoise was very angry with the leopard, and determined if possible to be revenged upon him. The tortoise, who was very clever, had discovered a shallow lake full of fish in the middle of the forest, and every morning he used to go to the lake and, without much trouble, bring back enough food for himself and his family.

One day the leopard met the tortoise and noticed how fat he was. As he was very thin himself he decided to watch the tortoise, so the next morning he hid himself in the long grass near the tortoise's house and waited very patiently, until the tortoise came along quite slowly, carrying a basket which appeared to be very heavy. Then the leopard sprang out, and said to the tortoise, "What have you got in that basket?"

The tortoise, as he did not want to lose his breakfast, replied that he was carrying firewood back to his home. Unfortunately for the tortoise the leopard had a very acute sense of smell, and knew at once that there was fish in the basket, so he said, "I know there is fish in there, and I am going to eat it."

The tortoise, not being in a position to refuse, as he was such a poor creature, said, "Very well. Let us sit down under this shady tree, and if you will make a fire I will go to my house and get pepper, oil, and salt, and then we will feed together."

To this the leopard agreed, and began to search about for dry wood, and started the fire. In the meantime the tortoise waddled off to his house, and very soon returned with the pepper, salt, and oil; he also brought a long piece of cane tie-tie, which is very strong. This he put on the ground, and began boiling the fish. Then he said to the leopard, "While we are waiting for the fish to cook, let us play at tying one another up to a tree. You may tie me up first, and when I say 'Tighten,' you must loosen the rope, and when I say 'Loosen,' you must tighten the rope."

The leopard, who was very hungry, thought that this game would make the time pass more quickly until the fish was cooked, so he said he would play. The tortoise then stood with his back to the tree and said, "Loosen the rope," and the leopard, in accordance with the rules of the game, began to tie up the tortoise. Very soon the tortoise shouted out, "Tighten!" and the leopard at once unfastened the tie-tie, and the tortoise was free.

The tortoise then said, "Now, leopard, it is your turn."

The leopard stood up against the tree and called out to the tortoise to loosen the rope, and the tortoise at once very quickly passed the rope several times round the leopard and got him fast to the tree. Then the leopard said, "Tighten the rope" but instead of playing the game in accordance with the rules he had laid down, the tortoise ran faster and faster with the rope round the leopard, taking great care, however, to keep out of reach of the leopard's claws, and very soon had the leopard so securely fastened that it was quite impossible for him to free himself.

All this time the leopard was calling out to the tortoise to let him go, as he was tired of the game, but the tortoise only laughed, and sat down at the fireside and commenced his meal. When he had finished he packed up the remainder of the fish for his family, and prepared to go, but before he started he said to the leopard, "You killed my mother and now you want to take my fish. It is not likely that I am going to the lake to get fish for you, so I shall leave you here to starve."

He then threw the remains of the pepper and salt into the leopard's eyes and quietly went on his way, leaving the leopard roaring with pain.

All that day and throughout the night the leopard was calling out for someone to release him, and vowing all sorts of vengeance on the tortoise, but no one came, as the people and animals of the forest do not like to hear the leopard's voice.

In the morning, when the animals began to go about to get their food, the leopard called out to everyone he saw to come and untie him, but they all refused, as they knew that if they did so the leopard would most likely kill them at once and eat them. At last a bush rat came near and saw the leopard tied up to the tree and asked him what was the matter, so the leopard told him that he had been playing a game of "tight" and "loose" with the tortoise, and that he had tied him up and left him there to starve.

The leopard then implored the bush rat to cut the ropes with his sharp teeth. The bush rat was very sorry for the leopard, but at the same time he knew that, if he let the leopard go, he would most likely be killed and eaten, so he hesitated, and said that he did not quite see his way to cutting the ropes. But this bush rat, being rather kind-hearted, and having had some experience of traps himself, could sympathise with the leopard in his uncomfortable position. He therefore thought for a time, and then hit upon a plan.

He first started to dig a hole under the tree, quite regardless of the leopard's cries. When he had finished the hole he came out and cut one of the ropes, and immediately ran into his hole, and waited there to see what would happen, but although the leopard struggled frantically, he could not get loose, as the tortoise had tied him up so fast. After a time, when he saw that there was no danger, the bush rat crept out again and very carefully bit through another rope, and then retired to his hole as before.

Again nothing happened, and he began to feel more confidence, so he bit several strands through one after the other until the leopard was free. The leopard, who was ravenous with hunger, instead of being grateful to the bush rat, directly he was free, made a dash at the bush rat with his big paw, but just missed him, as the bush rat had dived for his hole, but he was not quite quick enough to escape altogether, and the leopard's sharp claws scored his back and left marks which he carried to his grave.

Ever since then the bush rats have had white spots on their skins, which represent the marks of the leopard's claws.

TASKS DONE FOR A WIFE

This story has been edited and adapted from Robert Hamill Nassau's Where Animals Talk, first published in 1912 by Richard G. Badger at The Gorham Press, based out of Boston. This tale was originally told by storytellers from the Mpongwe tribe.

In the time when Mankind and all other Animals lived together, to all the Beasts the news came that there was a Merchant in a far country, who had a daughter, for whom he was seeking a marriage. And he had said, "I do not want money to be the dowry that shall be paid by a suitor for my daughter. But, whoever can complete some difficult challenges, which I shall assign him, then to him I will give her."

All the Beasts were competing for the prize.

First, Elephant went on that errand. The merchant said to him, "Do such-and-such tasks, and you shall have my daughter. More than that, I will give you wealth also." Elephant went at the tasks, tried, and failed, and came back saying he could not succeed.

Next, Gorilla stood up. He went and the merchant told him, in the same way as the Elephant, that he was to do certain tasks. Gorilla tried, and failed, and came back disgusted.

Then, Hippopotamus advanced, and said he would attempt to win the woman. His companions encouraged him with hopes of success, because of his size and strength. He went, tried, and failed.

Thus, almost all beasts attempted to meet the challenges, one after another. They tried to do the tasks, and failed.

At last there were left as contestants, only Leopard and Tortoise. Neither was disheartened by the failure of the others, for each asserted that he would succeed in marrying that rich daughter.

Tortoise said, "I'm going now!"

But Leopard said, "No! I first!"

Tortoise yielded, "Well, go. You are the elder. I will not compete with you. Go first!"

Leopard went, and made his application. The merchant said to him, "It is good that you have come. But, the others came, and failed."

Leopard said, "Very well."

He tried, and failed, and went back angry.

Tortoise then went. He saluted the merchant, and told him he had come to take his daughter. The merchant said, "Do so, but you must try to do the tasks first."

Tortoise tried all the tasks, and did them all. The first task concerned a calabash dipper that was cracked. The merchant said, "Take this cracked calabash and bring it to me full of water all the way from the spring to this town."

Tortoise looking and examining, objected, "This calabash is cracked! How can it carry water?"

The merchant replied, "You yourself must find out. If you succeed, you marry my daughter."

Tortoise took the calabash to the spring. Putting it into the water, he lifted it. But the water all ran out before he had gone a few steps. He did this five times and the water was always running out. Sitting, he meditated, "What is this? How can it be done?" Thinking again, he said, "I'll do it! I know how!"

He went to the forest, took gum of the Okume mahogany tree, lighted a fire, melted the gum, smeared it over the crack, and made it water-tight. Then, dipping the calabash into the spring, it did not leak. He took it full to the father-in-law, and called out, "Father-in-law! This is the calabash of water."

The merchant asked, "But what did you do to it?"

He answered "I mended it with gum."

The father said, "Good for you! The others did not think of that easy simple solution. You have sense!"

Tortoise then said, "I have finished this one task. Today has passed. Tomorrow I will begin on the other four."

The next morning, he came to receive his direction from the merchant, who said, "Ekaga! You see that tall tree far away? At the top are fruits. If you want my daughter, pluck the fruits from the top, and you shall marry her."

Tortoise went and stood watching and looking and examining the tree. Its trunk was all covered with soap, and impossible to be climbed. He returned to the merchant, and asked, "That fruit you wish, may it be obtained in any way, even if one does not climb the tree?"

He was answered, "Yes, in any way, except cutting down the tree. All I need is the fruit, and then I am satisfied."

Tortoise had already tried from morning to afternoon to climb that tree, but could not. So, after he had asked the merchant his question, he went back to the tree, and from evening, all night and until morning, he dug about the roots till they were all free. And the tree fell, without his having "cut" the trunk at all. So he took the fruit to the Merchant, and told him that he had not "cut down" the tree, but that he had it "dug up."

The merchant said, "You have done well. People who came before you failed to think of that. Good for you!"

On the third day, the merchant said to the spectators, "I will not name the other three tasks. You, my assistants, may name them."

So they thought of one task after another. But one and another said, "No, that is not hard. Let us search for a harder task." Finally, they found three hard tasks. Tortoise was ready for and accomplished them all.

Then the merchant announced, "Now, you may marry my daughter, and tomorrow you shall make your journey." They made a great feast. An ox was killed, and they had songs and music all night, clear on till morning.

But, while all this was going on, Leopard, who was back at his town, was saying to himself, "This Ekaga! He has stayed five days! Had he failed, he would not have stayed so long! So! He has been able to do the tasks! Is that a good thing?"

On the day that Tortoise started on the journey to seek the merchant's daughter, Leopard had been heard to say, "If Ekaga succeeds in getting that wife, I will take her from him by force."

When Tortoise was ready to start on his return journey with his wife, the father-in-law gave him very many things, slaves and goats and a variety of goods, and said, "Go, you and your wife and these things. I send people to escort you part of the way. They are not to go clear on to your town, but are to turn back on the way."

Tortoise and the great company journeyed on. When the escort were about to turn back, Tortoise said, "Day is past. Make a camp here. We sleep here and, in the morning you shall go back."

That night he thought, "Njegâ said he would rob me of my wife. Perhaps he may come to meet me on the way!" So, he swallowed all of the things, to hide them, wife, servants, and all.

While Tortoise was on his way, Leopard had set out to meet him. So, in the morning, the two, journeying in opposite directions, met. Tortoise gave Leopard a respectful "Mbolo!" and Leopard returned the salutation.

Leopard asked, "What news? That woman, have you married her?"

Tortoise answered, "That woman! Not at all!"

Leopard, seeing that Tortoise's style and manner was that of one proud with success, said, "Surely you have married, for you look happy, and show signs of success."

But Tortoise swore he had not married.

Leopard only said, "Good."

Then Tortoise asked, "But, where are you going?"

Leopard answered, "I am going out walking and hunting. But you, where are you going?"

Tortoise replied, "I did not succeed in marrying the woman, so I am going back to town. I tried, but I failed."

"But," said Leopard, "what then makes your belly so big?"

Tortoise replied, "On the way I found an abundance of mushrooms, and I ate heartily of them. If you do not believe it, I can show you them by vomiting them up."

Leopard said, "Never mind your vomit. Go on your journey."

And Leopard went on his way. But, soon he thought, "Ah! Ekaga has lied to me!" So he ran around back, and came forward to meet Tortoise again.

Tortoise looked and saw Leopard coming, and observed that his face was full of wrath. He was afraid, but said to himself, "If I flee, Njegâ will catch me. I will go forward and try artifice."

As he approached Leopard, the latter was very angry, and said, "You play with me! You say you have not married the woman I wanted. Tell me the truth!"

Tortoise again swore an oath, "No! I have not married the woman! I told you I ate mushrooms, and offered to show you, and you refused."

So Leopard said, "Well, then, vomit."

Tortoise bent over, and vomited and vomited mushrooms and mushrooms, and then said triumphantly, "So! Njegâ you see!"

Leopard looked, and said, "But, Ekaga, your belly is still full. Go on vomiting."

Tortoise tried to excuse himself, "I have done vomiting."

Leopard persisted, "No, keep on at it."

Tortoise went on retching and a box of goods fell out of his mouth.

Leopard still said, "Go on!" and Tortoise vomited in succession a table and other furniture. He was compelled to go on retching, and slaves came out. And at last, up was vomited the woman!

Leopard shouted, "Ah! Ekaga! You lied! You said you had not married! I will take this woman!" And he took her, sarcastically saying, "Ekaga, you have done me a good work! You have brought me all these things, these goods, and slaves, and a wife! Thank you!"

Tortoise thought to himself, "I have no strength for war." So, though anger was in his heart, he showed no displeasure in his face. And they all went on together toward their town. With wrath still in his heart, he went clear on to the town, and then made his complaint to each of the townspeople. But they all were afraid of Leopard, and said nothing, nor dared to give Tortoise even sympathy.

There was in that country among the mountains, an enormous Goat. The other beasts, all except Leopard, were accustomed to go to that Goat, when hungry, and say, "We have no meat to eat." And the Goat allowed them to cut pieces of flesh from his body. He could let any part of the interior of his body be taken except his heart. All the Animals had agreed among themselves not to tell Leopard where they got their meat, lest he, in his greediness, would go and take the heart. So they had told him they got their meat as he did, hunting.

Tortoise, angry because Leopard has taken his wife, said to himself, "I will make a cause of complaint against Njegâ that shall bring punishment upon him from our King. I will cause Njegâ to kill that Goat."

On another day, Tortoise went and got meat from the Goat, and came back to town, and did not hide it from Leopard. Leopard said to him, "Ekaga! Where did you get this meat?"

Tortoise whispered, "Come to my house, and I will tell you." They went. And Tortoise divided the meat with him, and said, "Do not tell on me, but, we get the meat off at a great Goat. Tomorrow, I'll go and you follow behind me."

So, the next day, they went, Tortoise as if by himself, and Leopard following, off to the great Goat. Once they had arrived, Leopard wondered at the sight, "Oh! This great Goat! But, from where do you take its meat?"

Tortoise replied, "Wait for me! You will see!" He went, and Leopard followed. Tortoise said to the Goat, "We have meat-hunger and we come to seek meat from you."

The Goat's mouth was open as usual. Tortoise entered, and Leopard followed, to get flesh from inside. In the Goat's interior was a house, full of meat, and they entered it. Leopard wondered at its size, and Tortoise told him, "Cut where you please, but not from the heart, lest the Goat die." And they began to take meat. Leopard, with greediness, coveting the forbidden heart, went up to it with his knife.

Tortoise exclaimed, "There! There! Be careful."

But Leopard, though he had enough other flesh, longed for the heart, and was not satisfied. He again approached the heart with the knife and Tortoise warned and protested. These very prohibitions caused Leopard to want his own way, and his greediness overcame him. He cut the heart: and the Goat fell dying.

Tortoise exclaimed, "Eh! Njegâ! I told you not to touch the heart! Because of this matter I will inform on you." And he added, "Since it is so, let us go."

But Leopard said, "Goat's mouth is shut. How shall we get out? Let us hide in this house." And he asked, "Where will you hide?"

Tortoise replied, "In the stomach."

Leopard said, "Stomach! It is the very thing for me, Njegâ, myself!"

So Ekaga consented, "Well! Take it! I will hide in the gall-bladder." So they hid, each in his place.

Soon, as they listened, they heard voices shouting, "The Goat is dead! A fearful thing! The Goat is dead!"

That news spread, and all who had been accustomed to get flesh there, came to see what was the matter. They all said that, as the Goat was dead, it was best to cut and divide him. They slit open the belly, and said, "Lay aside this big stomach for it is good, but throw away the bitter gall-sac."

They looked for the heart, but there was none! A child, to whom the gall-bladder had been handed so that he could throw it away, was flinging it into some bushes. As he did so, out jumped something from among the bushes and the child asked, "Who are you?"

The thing replied, pretending to be vexed, "I am Ekaga. I came here with the others to get meat, and you, just as I arrived, threw that dirty thing in my face!"

The other people pacified him, "Do not get angry. Excuse the child. He did not see you. You shall have your share."

Then Tortoise called out, "Silence! Silence! Silence!"

They all stood ready to listen, and he said, "Do not cut up the Goat till we first know who killed it. That stomach there! What makes it so big?"

Leopard, in the stomach, heard but he did not believe that Tortoise meant it, and thought to himself, "What a fool is this Ekaga, in pretending to inform on me, by directing attention to the stomach!"

Tortoise ordered, "All of you, take your spears, and stick that stomach! For the one who killed Goat is in it!" And they all got their spears ready.

Leopard did not speak or move; for, he still thought Tortoise was only joking. Tortoise began with his spear, and the others all thrust their spears in too. And Leopard holding the heart, was seen dying!

All shouted, "Ah! Njegâ killed our Goat! Ah, he's the one who killed it."

Tortoise taunted Leopard, "Asai! Shame on you. You took my wife and now you are dead!"

Leopard died. They divided the Goat, and returned to town. Tortoise took again his wife and all his goods, now that Leopard was dead. And he was satisfied that his artifice had surpassed Leopard's strength.

"EZIWO DIED OF SLEEP": A PROVERB

This story has been edited and adapted from Robert Hamill Nassau's Where Animals Talk, first published in 1912 by Richard G. Badger at The Gorham Press, based out of Boston. This tale was originally told by storytellers from the Mpongwe tribe.

Antelope and Ox went to a town to dance Bweti, which is a type of spirit-dance. After the dance, Antelope, exhausted with the exercise, fell asleep in the Bweti-house. While he was there, certain persons made a plot to kill him. Ox heard of it, and came to warn him, calling gently in case he should be overheard and himself seized, "Njiwo! Eziwo!" But antelope did not hear, and Ox made no further effort, and ran away to his home in fear for his own life.

Then Antelope's wife came while he still slept and loudly called him. He, only half-awake, grumbled, "What do you call me for? Let me rest. I'm tired from the dancing."

She persisted, "I call you because certain persons want to kill you."

But, he, still heavy with sleep, did not understand, and was not willing to rise, and went on sleeping. Then his wife, unable to arouse him, went to call other people to help her.

While she was away, his enemies came and tied him with ropes, and left him there, still sleeping, alone in the house. They locked the house, and went away, intending to return and kill him when he should awake. Before they came back, his wife returned with aid, and, with machetes and knives, they cut open the door, and found Antelope with his limbs tied, and still sleeping. They roughly shook him, and he, half-conscious, asked, "What do you want here?"

His wife replied, "I have come to carry you away." So, she untied the ropes, and they lifted him and carried him away, still too sleepy to walk himself.

While all this was going on, the people of the town to which Ox had fled, asked him, "There were two of you who went to dance Bweti. You are here, but where is the other?"

Ox, assuming that Antelope was dead, and not knowing what Antelope's wife had done, told how he had been unable to waken him, and said, "Eziwo was killed while asleep."

Then the village people said regretfully, "Eh! Eziwo! Sleep has killed him!"

In the meantime, Antelope and his wife had reached the town, where the news of his death had preceded them, and the people wondered, saying, "Nyare reported that you were cut to pieces!" Then Antelope's wife explained that he would have been killed, because Ox had not made every effort to arouse him from his deep sleep.

So the friendship of Ox and Antelope ended. And the proverb came, that, "Eziwo died of sleep."

DO NOT TRUST YOUR FRIEND

This story has been edited and adapted from Robert Hamill Nassau's Where Animals Talk, first published in 1912 by Richard G. Badger at The Gorham Press, based out of Boston. This tale was originally told by storytellers from the Mpongwe tribe.

At a time long ago, the Animals were living in the Forest together. Most of them were at peace with each other. But Leopard was discovered to be a bad person. All the other animals refused to be friendly with him. Also, Wild Rat, a small animal, was found out to be a deceiver.

One day, Rat went to visit Leopard, who politely gave him a chair, and Rat sat down. "Mbolo!" "Ai, Mbolo!" each saluted to the other. Leopard said to his visitor, "What's the news?"

Rat replied, "Njegâ! News is bad. In all the villages I passed through, in coming today, your name is only ill-spoken of, people saying, 'Njegâ is bad! Njegâ is bad!'"

Leopard replied, "Yes, you do not lie. People say truly that Njegâ is bad. But, look, Ntori, I, Njegâ, am an evil one, but my badness comes from other animals. Because, when I go out to visit, there is no one who salutes me. When anyone sees me, he flees with fear. But, for what does he fear me? I have not vexed him. So, I pursue the one that fears me. I want to ask him, 'Why do you fear me?' But, when I pursue it, it goes on fleeing more rapidly. So, I become angry, wrath rises in my heart, and if I overtake it, I kill it on the spot. One reason why I am bad is that. If the animals would speak to me properly, and not flee from me, then, Ntori, I would not kill them. See! You, Ntori, have I seized you?"

Rat replied, "No."

Then Leopard said, "Then, Ntori, come near to this table, that we may talk well."

Rat, because of his subtlety and caution, when he took the chair given him on his arrival, had placed it near the door.

Leopard repeated, "Come near to the table."

Rat excused himself, "Never mind. I am comfortable here and I came here today to tell you that it is not well for a person to be without friends, and, I, Ntori, I say to you, let us be friends."

Leopard said, "Very good!"

But now, even after this compact of friendship, Rat told falsehoods about Leopard, who, not knowing this, often had conversations with him, and would confide to him all the thoughts of his heart. For example, Leopard would say to Rat, "Tomorrow I am going to hunt Ngowa, and next day I will go to hunt Nkambi," or whatever the animal was. And Rat, at night, would go to Hog or to Antelope or the other animal, and say, "Give me pay, and I will tell you a secret." They would lay down to him his price. And then he would tell them, "Be careful tomorrow. I heard that Njegâ was coming to kill you." The same night, Rat would secretly return to his own house, and lie down as if he had not been out.

Then, next day, when Leopard would go out hunting, the Animals were prepared and full of caution, to watch for his coming. Leopard could find none of them, for they were all hidden. Leopard thus often went to the forest, and came back empty-handed. There was no meat for him to eat, and he had to eat only leaves of the trees. He said to himself, "I will not sit down and look for explanation to come to me. I will myself find out the reason for this. For, I, Njegâ, I should eat flesh and drink blood, and here I have come down to eating the food of goats, such as grass and leaves."

So, in the morning, Leopard went to the great doctor Ra-Marânge, and said, "I have come to you, I, Njegâ. For these five or six months I have been unable to kill an animal. But, cause me to know the reason of this."

Ra-Marânge took his looking-glass and his harp, and struck the harp, and looked at the glass. Then he laughed aloud, "Ke, ke, ke."

Leopard asked, "Ra-Marânge, for what reason do you laugh?"

He replied, "I laugh, because this matter is a small affair. You, Njegâ, so big and strong, you do not know this little thing!"

Leopard acknowledged, "Yes, I have not been able to find it out."

Ra-Marânge said, "Tell me the names of your friends."

Leopard answered "I have no friends. Nkambi dislikes me, Nyare refuses me, Ngowa the same. Of all animals, none are friendly to me."

Ra-Marânge said, "Not so. Think exactly. Think again."

Leopard was silent and thought, and then said, "Yes, truly, I have one friend, Ntori."

The Doctor said, "But, look! If you find a friend, it is not well to tell him all the thoughts of your heart. If you tell him two or three, leave the rest. Do not tell him all. But, you, Njegâ, you consider that Ntori is your friend, and you show him all the thoughts of your heart. But, do you know the heart of Ntori, how it is inside? Look at what he does! If you let him know that you are going next day to kill this and that, then he starts out at night, and goes to inform those animals, 'So-and-so, said Njegâ, but, be you on your guard.' Now, look! If you wish to be able to kill other animals, first kill Ntori."

Leopard was surprised, "Ngâ! Ntori lies to me?"

Ra-Marânge said, "Yes."

So, Leopard returned to his town. And he sent a child to call Rat. Rat came. Leopard said, "Ntori! These days you have not come to see me. Where have you been?"

Rat replied, "I was sick."

Leopard said, "I called you today to sit at my table to eat."

Rat excused himself, "Thanks! But the sickness is still in my body; I will not be able to eat." And he went away.

Whenever Rat visited or spoke to Leopard, he did not enter the house, but sat on a chair by the door. Leopard sent for him daily and he came, but constantly refrained from entering the house.

Leopard said in his heart, "Ntori does not approach near to me, but sits by the door. How shall I catch him?" Thinking and thinking, he called his wife, and said, "I have found a plan by which to kill Ntori. Tomorrow, I will lie down in the street, and you cover my body with a cloth as corpses are covered. Wear an old ragged cloth, and take ashes and mark your body, as in mourning, and go out on the road wailing, saying, 'Njegâ is dead! Njegâ, the friend of Ntori is dead!' And, for Ntori, when he comes as a friend to the mourning, put his chair by me, and say, 'Sit there near your friend.' When he sits on that chair, I will jump up and kill him there."

His wife replied, "Very good!"

Next morning, Leopard, lying down in the street, pretended that he was dead. His wife dressed herself in worn-out clothes, and smeared her face, and went clear on to Rat's village, wailing "Ah! Njegâ is dead! Ntori's friend is dead!"

Rat asked her, "But, Njegâ died of what disease? Yesterday, I saw him looking well, and today comes word that he is dead!"

The wife answered, "Yes: Njegâ died without disease. He was just cut off! I wonder at the matter. I came to call you, for you were his friend. So, as is your duty as a man, go there and help bury the corpse in the jungle."

Rat and Leopard's wife went together, and there was Leopard stretched out as a corpse! Rat asked the wife, "What is this matter? Njegâ! Is he really dead?"

She replied, "Yes. I told you so. Here is a chair for you to sit near your friend."

Rat, being cautious, had not sat on the chair, but stood off, as he wailed, "Ah! Njegâ is dead! Ah! My friend is dead!" Rat then called out, "Wife of Njegâ! Njegâ, he was a great person, but did he not tell you any sign by which it might be known, according to custom, that he was really dead?"

She replied, "No, he did not tell me."

Rat went on to speak, "You, Njegâ, when you were living and we were friends, you told me in confidence, saying, 'When I, Njegâ, shall die, I will lift my arm upward, and you will know that I am really dead.' But, let us cease the wailing and stop crying. I will try the test on Njegâ, whether he is dead! Lift your arm!"

Leopard lifted his arm. Rat, in his heart, laughed, "Ah! Njegâ is not dead!" But, he proceeded, "Njegâ! Njegâ! You said, if you were really dead, you would shake your body. Shake if it is so!"

Leopard shook his whole body. Rat said openly, "Ah! Njegâ is dead indeed! He shook his body!"

The wife said, "But, as you say he is dead, here is the chair for you, as chief friend, to sit on by him."

Rat said, "Yes. But wait for me; I will go off a little while, and will come back soon."

Leopard, lying on the ground, and hearing this, knew in his heart, "Ah! Ntori wants to flee from me! I will wait no longer!" Up he jumped to seize Rat, who, being too quick for him, fled away. Leopard pursued him with leaps and jumps so rapidly that he almost caught him. Rat got to his hole in the ground just in time to rush into it. But his tail was sticking out, and Leopard, looking down the hole, seized the tail.

Rat called out, "You have not caught me, as you think! What you are holding is a rootlet of a tree."

Leopard let go of the tail. Rat switched it in after him, and jeered at Leopard, "You had hold of my tail! And you have let it go! You will not catch me again!"

Leopard, in a rage, said, "You will have to show me the way by which you will emerge from this hole; for you will never come out of it alive!"

THE EAR OF CORN AND THE TWELVE MEN

This story has been edited and adapted from the appendix of George Webbe Dasent's Popular Tales From The Norse, first published in 1907 by Edmonston and Douglas, based out of Edinburgh, Scotland.

Anansi said to the King, that if he would give him an ear of corn, he would bring him twelve strong men. The King gave him the ear of corn, and Anansi went away. At last he got to a house, where he asked for a night's lodging which was given him. The next morning he got up very early, and threw the ear of corn out of the door to the fowls, and went back to bed. When he got up later in the morning, he looked for his ear of corn, and could not find it anywhere, so he told them he was sure the fowls had eaten it, and he would not be satisfied unless they gave him the best cock they had.

So they were obliged to give him the cock, and he went away with it, all day, until night, when he came to another house, and asked again for a night's lodging, which he got, but when they wanted to put the cock into the fowl-house, he said no, the cock must sleep in the pen with the sheep, so they put the cock with the sheep. At midnight he got up, killed the cock, threw it back into the pen, and went back to bed.

Next morning when it was time for him to go away, his cock was dead, and he would not take anything for it but one of the best sheep, so they gave it to him, and he went off with it all that day, until night-fall, when he got to a village, where he again asked for a night's lodging, which was given to him, and when they wanted to put his sheep with the other sheep, he said, no, the sheep must sleep with the cattle. They put the sheep with the cattle. In the middle of the night he got up and killed the sheep, and went back to bed. Next morning he went for his sheep, which was dead, so he told them they must give him the best heifer for his sheep, and if they would not do so, he would go back and tell the King, who would come and make war on them.

So to get rid of him, they were glad to give him the heifer, and let him go, and away he went, and walked nearly all day with the heifer. Towards evening he met a funeral, and asked whose it was? One of the men said, it was his sister, so he asked the men if they would let him have her. They said no, but after a while, he begged so hard, saying he would give them the heifer, that they consented, and he took the dead body and walked away, carrying it until it was dark, when he came to a large town, where he went to a house and begged hard for a night's lodging for himself and his sister, who was so tired he was obliged to carry her, and they would be thankful if they would let them rest there that night.

So they let them in, and he asked them to let them sit in the dark, as his sister could not bear the light. So they took them into a room, and left them in the dark, and when they were alone, Anansi seated himself on a bench near the table, and put his sister close by his side, with his arm round her to keep her up. Presently they brought them in some supper, with one plate he set before his sister, and he put her hand in it. The other plate was set for Anansi, but he ate out of both plates. When it was time to go to bed, he asked if they would allow his sister to sleep in a room where there were twelve strong men sleeping, for she had fits, and if she had one in the night, they would be able to hold her, and would not disturb the rest of the house.

So they agreed to this, and he carried her in his arms, because, he said she was so tired, she was asleep, and laid her in a bed. He charged the men not to disturb her, and went himself to sleep in the next room. In the middle of the night he heard the men calling out, for they smelt a horrid smell, and tried to wake the woman. First one man gave her a blow, and then another, until all the men had struck her, but Anansi took no notice of the noise. In the morning when he went in for his sister and found her dead, he declared they had killed her, and that he must have the twelve men. To this the townsmen said no, not supposing that all the men had killed her, but the men confessed that they had each given her a blow-so he would not be satisfied with less than the twelve, and he carried them off to the King, and delivered them up.

WHICH IS THE FATTEST?

This story has been edited and adapted from Robert Hamill Nassau's Where Animals Talk, first published in 1912 by Richard G. Badger at The Gorham Press, based out of Boston. This tale was originally told by storytellers from the Mpongwe tribe.

Ra-Mborakinda was dwelling in his Town, with his people and the glory of his Kingdom. There were gathered there the Manatus, the Oyster and the Hog, waiting to be assigned their kingdoms. To pass the time, while waiting until the King should summon them for their assignments, Oyster said, "You, Manga, and Ngowa, let us have a dance!" And they went to exhibit their best dances before the King. They danced and danced, each one dancing his own special dance.

After that they made a fire, each one at his own fire-place, and sat down to rest. Then Hog proposed a new entertainment. He said, "You, Arandi, and Manga, we all three shall test ourselves by fire, to see who has the most fat." And they all three went into their respective fire-places, Hog into his, and Manatus into his, and Oyster into its. Under the influence of the heat, the fat in their bodies began to melt.

Then the King announced, "To the one who shall prove to have the most fat, I will give a great extent of country as its kingdom." So, they all three tried to show much fat, in their effort to win the prize.

Presently, the fat of Hog began to stop flowing, for he had not a great deal. As to Oyster, it had no fat. What it produced was not fat at all, but water, and that was in such quantity that it put out its fire.

These facts about the Hog and Oyster were reported to the King, and when he inquired how Manatus was getting on, it was found that she had such abundance of fat, that the oil flowing from her had burst into flame and had set the town on fire.

At this, the King wondered, and exclaimed, "This Manga, that lives in the water, has yet enough fat to set the town afire!"

Then Manatus with Hog and Oyster went and sat together in the open court before the King's house, to await his decision. When he was ready, he sent two heralds to summon not only those three, but all the Tribes of the Beasts of the Forest, and of the Fishes of the Sea, and the town was full of these visitors. But, Hog and all his tribe had become impatient and had gone off for a walk. All the other animals that had been summoned, came into the King's presence, and he, having ascended his throne, said, "I am ready now to speak with these three persons, but, I see that the Ingowa are not here. So, because of their disrespect in going off to amuse themselves with a walk instead of waiting for me, I condemn them and they shall no longer wear any horns."

Then the King announced that, as Manatus had the most fat, her promised territory should be the Sea, and of it she should be ruler. But, Manatus said, "I do not want to live in the Sea, in case I be killed there."

The King asked, "Then, where will you prefer to live?"

She answered, "In such rivers as I shall like."

That is the reason that the Manatus lives only in rivers and bays. For, one day she and her children had floated with the tide to the mouth of a river and into the Sea, and some of them had been killed there by sharks and other big fish. So, the Manatus is never now found near the Sea on ordinary tides, but only when high tides have swept it down.

Just as the King had made his announcement, the company of Hogs returned and entered the Assembly. They explained, "We have just come back from our walk, and we wish to resume our horns which we left here."

But the King refused, and kept possession of the horns.

Hog begged, "Please! let me have my horns!"

But the King swore an oath, saying, "By the Blessing! Wherever you go, and whatever you be, you shall have no horns."

So the Hogs departed.

Now Oyster stood up, and said, "I wish to go to my place. Where shall it be?"

The King said, "I will give you no other place than what you already have had. I do not wish to put you into the fresh-water springs and brooks with Manga. You shall go into the salty waters."

So Oyster went, and its race lives on the edge of the rivers, near the Sea, in brackish waters. And the King said to Oyster, "All the tribes of Mankind, by the Sea, when they fail to obtain other fish, shall be allowed to eat you."

All knew that this was a punishment given by the King to Oyster, for having dared the test by fire, pretending that it had fat, when it had none.

HOW ANANSI'S HIND BECAME BIG, AND HOW HIS HEAD BECAME SMALL

This story has been edited and adapted from Captain R. S. Rattray's Akan-Ashanti Folk-Tales, first published in 1930 by Oxford University Press – American Branch, New York.

One day, a famine came and Kwaku Anansi told his family that he'd search for food so they could eat. He soon went to a stream and met some people, who he discovered were spirits. The spirits were draining the water in the hope that they would be able to catch some fish to eat. Anansi was intrigued and asked if he could join them, and the spirits in turn gave him their permission. The spirits were using their skulls to drain the river, and when Anansi approached, the spirits asked if they could remove his as well. Anansi said they could, and they did so, giving him his skull so that he could join them.

While they drained the water, the spirits sang a beautiful song: "We, the Spirits, when we splash the river-bed dry to catch fish, we use our heads to splash the water. Oh, the Spirits, we are splashing the water."

The song intrigued Anansi and he asked if he could sing it also. They allowed him, and together they continued to sing until they finally drained some of the stream. The spirits gave Anansi his own share of fish in a basket and restored his skull, but warned him never to sing the song again on that day, or his skull would open and fall off again. Anansi said that he had no reason to sing it again, because they'd given him more than enough to eat and he wanted nothing else. The Spirits bade him farewell, and Anansi went away. The spirits soon left, and went elsewhere to catch more fish.

Soon, the spirits began singing their song again, and Anansi eventually heard it. He began to sing it again, and as soon as he finished, his skull fell off again like they'd warned him. Anansi picked his skull up in embarrassment and cried out to the spirits that his head had fallen off. The spirits heard him, and decided to return to him, to hear him explain himself. Anansi begged them for help and apologized to them, asking them to restore his skull. The spirits said they would, but warned Anansi that if he disobeyed them again, they would not return to help him, and bade him leave before heading off on their own. Yet, just as soon as they'd left, Anansi heard them singing their song and repeated it himself.

Anansi's skull detached and fell again, having disobeyed the spirits another time. Before it hit the ground, he caught it with his rear-end and he fled from the riverside. So it is that Anansi has a small head and a large bottom, because of his hard-headedness.

LEOPARD OF THE FINE SKIN

This story has been edited and adapted from Robert Hamill Nassau's Where Animals Talk, first published in 1912 by Richard G. Badger at The Gorham Press, based out of Boston. This tale was originally told by storytellers from the Mpongwe tribe.

At the town of Ra-Mborakinda, where he lived with his wives and his children and his glory, this occurred.

He had a beloved daughter, by name Ilâmbe. He loved her very much and sought to please her in many ways, and gave her many servants to serve her. When she grew up to womanhood, she said that she did not wish anyone to come to ask for her hand in marriage. She said that she herself would choose a husband. "Moreover, I will never marry any man who has even the slightest blotch on his skin."

Her father did not like her to speak in that way, but nevertheless, he did not forbid her.

When men began to come to the father and say, "I desire your daughter Ilâmbe for a wife," he would say, "Go, and ask herself."

Then when the man went to Ilâmbe's house, and would say, "I have come to ask for you in marriage," her only reply was a question, "Have you a clear skin, and no blotches on your body?" If he answered, "Yes," Ilâmbe would say, "But, I must see for myself; come into my room." There she required the man to take off all his clothing. And if, on examination, she saw the slightest pimple or scar, she would point toward it, and say, "That! I do not want you." Then perhaps he would begin to plead, "All my skin is right, except..." But she would interrupt him, "No! for even that little mark I do not want you."

So it went on with all who came, she finding fault with even a small pimple or scar. And all suitors were rejected. The news spread abroad that Ra-Mborakinda had a beautiful daughter, but that no one was able to obtain her, because of what she said about diseases of the skin. Still, many tried to obtain her. Even animals changed themselves to human form, and sought her, in vain.

At last, Leopard said, "Ah! This beautiful woman! I hear about her beauty, and that no one is able to get her. I think I better take my turn, and try. But, first I will go to Ra-Marânge."

He went to that magic-doctor, and told his story about Ra-Mborakinda's fine daughter, and how no man could get her because of her fastidiousness about skins. Ra-Marânge told him, "I am too old. I do not now do those things about medicines. Go to Ogula-ya-mpazya-vazya."

So, Leopard went to him. As usual, the sorcerer Ogula jumped into his fire, and coming out with power, directed Leopard to tell what he wanted. So he told the whole story again, and asked how he should obtain the clean body of a man. The sorcerer prepared for him a great "medicine" by which to give him a human body, tall, graceful, strong and clean. Leopard then went back to his town, told his people his plans, and prepared their bodies also for a change if needed. Having taken also a human name, Ogula, he then went to Ra-Mborakinda, saying, "I wish your daughter Ilâmbe for my wife."

On his arrival, at Ra-Mborakinda's, the people admired the stranger, and felt sure that Ilâmbe would accept this suitor, exclaiming, "This fine-looking man! His face! And his gait! And his body!"

When he had made his request of Ra-Mborakinda, he was told, as usual, to go to Ilâmbe and see whether she would like him. When he went to her house, he looked so handsome, that Ilâmbe was at once pleased with him. He told her, "I love you and I come to marry you. You have refused many. I know the reason why, but I think you will be satisfied with me."

She replied, "I think you have heard from others the reason why I refuse men. I will see whether you have what I want." And she added, "Let us go into the room and let me see your skin."

They entered the room and Ogula-Njegâ removed his fine clothing. Ilâmbe examined him with close scrutiny from his head to his feet. She found not the slightest scratch or mark. His skin was like a babe's. Then she said, "Yes! This is my man! Truly! I love you, and will marry you!"

She was so pleased with her acquisition, that she remained in the room enjoying again a minute examination of her husband's beautiful skin. Then she went out, and ordered her servants to cook food, prepare water and drinks for him, and he did not go out of the house, nor have a longing to go back to his town, for he found that he was loved.

On the third day, he went to tell the father, Ra-Mborakinda, that he was ready to take his wife off to his town. Ra-Mborakinda consented. All that day, they prepared food for the marriage-feast. But, all the while that this man-beast, Ogula-Njegâ was there, Ra-Mborakinda, by his okove, by his magic fetish, knew that some evil would come out of this marriage. However, as Ilâmbe had insisted on choosing her own way, he did not interfere.

After the marriage was over, and the feast eaten, Ra-Mborakinda called his daughter, and said, "Ilâmbe, mine, now you are going off on your journey."

She said, "Yes, for I love my husband."

The father asked, "Do you love him truly?"

She answered "Yes."

Then he told her, "As you are married now, you need a present from me for your ozendo, for your bridal gift." So, he gave her a few presents, and told her, "Go to that house," indicating a certain house in the town, and he gave her the key of the house, and told her to go and open the door. That was the house where he kept all his charms for war, and fetishes of all kinds. He told her, "When you go in, you will see two Kabala, standing side by side. The one that will look a little dull, with its eyes directed to the ground, take it, and leave the brighter looking one. When you are coming with it, you will see that it walks a little lame. Nevertheless, take it."

She objected, "But, father, why do you not give me the finer one, and not the weak one?"

But he said, "No!" and made a knowing smile, as he repeated, "Go, and take the one I tell you."

He had reason for giving this one. The finer-looking one had only fine looks, but this other one would someday save her by its intelligence.

She went and took Horse, and returned to her father, and the journey was prepared. The father sent her, servants to carry the baggage, and who would remain with and work for her at the town of her marriage. She and her husband arranged all their things, and said good-bye, and off they went, both of them sitting on Horse's back.

They journeyed and they journeyed. On the way, Ogula-Njegâ, though felt the calling of his natural form and skin, and he started to want his old tastes. Having been so many days without tasting blood or uncooked meats, as they passed through the forest of wild beasts, the old longing came on him. They emerged onto a great prairie, and journeyed across it toward another forest. Before they had entirely crossed the prairie, the longing for his prey so overcame him that he said, "Wife, you with your Kabala and the servants stay here while I go rapidly ahead. Wait for me until I come again."

So he went off, entered the forest, and changed himself back to Leopard. He hunted for prey, caught a small animal, and ate it, and another, and ate it. After being satisfied, he washed his hands and mouth in a brook, and, changing again to human form, he returned to the prairie and to his wife.

She observed him closely, and saw a hard, strange look on his face. She said, "But, all this while! What have you been doing?" He made an excuse. They went on.

And the next day, it was the same, he leaving her, and telling her to wait till he returned, and hunting and eating as a Leopard. Ilâmbe was ignorant of all these goings on, but Horse knew. He would speak after a while, but was not ready yet.

So it went on, until they came to Leopard's town. Before they reached it, Ogula-Njegâ, by the preparations he had first made, had changed his mother into a human form in which to welcome his wife. Also the few people of the town, all with human forms, welcomed her. But, they did not sit much with her. They stayed in their own houses, and Ogula-Njegâ and his wife stayed in theirs. For a few days, Leopard tried to be a pleasant Ogula, deceiving his wife. But his taste for blood was still in his heart. He began to say, "I am going to another town. I have business there." And off he would go, hunting as a leopard. When he returned, it would be late in the day. He did this on all of the other days.

After a time, Ilâmbe wished to make a food-plantation, and sent her men-servants to clear the ground. Ogula-Njegâ would go around in the forest on the edge of the plantation and catch one of the men, meaning that on those days there would return one servant less. One by one, all the men-servants went missing, and it was not known what became of them, except that Leopard's people knew. One night Ogula-Njegâ was out and, he met one of the female servants. She too was later reported missing.

Sometimes, when Ogula-Njegâ was away, Ilâmbe, feeling lonesome, would go and pet Horse. After the loss of this maid-servant, Horse thought it was time to warn Ilâmbe of what was going on. While she was petting him, he said, "Eh! Ilâmbe! You do not see the trouble that is coming to you!"

She asked, "What trouble?"

He exclaimed, "What trouble? If your father had not sent me with you, what would have become of you? Where are all your servants that you brought with you? You do not know where they go to, but I know. Do you think that they disappear without a reason? I will tell you where they go. It is your man who eats them. It is he who wastes them!"

She could not believe it, and argued, "Why should he destroy them?"

Horse replied, "If you doubt it, wait for the day when your last remaining servant is gone."

Two days after that, at night, another maid-servant disappeared. Another day passed. On another day, Ogula-Njegâ went off to hunt beasts, with the intention that, if he failed to get any, at night he would eat his wife.

When he had gone, Ilâmbe, in her loneliness, went to fondle Horse. He said to her, "Did I not tell you? The last maid is gone. You yourself will be the next one. I will give you counsel. When you have opportunity this night, prepare yourself ready to run away. Get yourself a large gourd, and fill it with ground-nuts. Get another and fill it with gourd-seeds, and another with water." He told her to bring these things to him, and he would know the best time to start.

While they were talking, Leopard's mother was out in the street, and heard the two voices. She said to herself, "Ilâmbe, wife of my son, does she talk with Kabala as if it was a person?" But, she said nothing to Ilâmbe, nor asked her about it.

Night came on and Ogula-Njegâ returned. He said nothing but his face looked hard and bad. Ilâmbe was troubled and somewhat frightened by his ugly looks. So, at night, on retiring, she began to ask him, "But why? Has anything displeased you?"

He answered, "No. I am not troubled about anything. Why do you ask questions?"

"Because I see it in your face that your countenance is not pleasant."

"No, there's no matter. Everything is right. Only, about my business, I think I must start very early." Ogula-Njegâ had begun to think, "Now she is suspecting me. I think I will not eat her this night, but will put it off until the next night."

That night, Ilâmbe did not sleep. In the morning, Leopard said that he would go to his business, but would come back soon. When he was gone away to his hunting work, Ilâmbe felt lonesome, and went to Horse. He, thinking this a good time to run away, they started at once, without letting anyone in the village know, and taking with them the three gourds. Horse said that they must go quickly, for, Leopard, when he discovered them gone, would rapidly pursue. So they went fast and faster, Horse looking back from time to time to see whether Leopard was pursuing.

After they had been gone quite a while, Ogula-Njegâ returned from his business to his village, went into his house, and did not see Ilâmbe. He called to his mother, "Where is Ilâmbe?"

His mother answered, "I saw Ilâmbe with her Kabala, talking together. They have been at it for two days."

Ogula-Njegâ began to search, and, seeing the hoof-prints, he exclaimed, "Mi asaiya. Shame for me! Ilâmbe has run away, but we shall meet today!"

He instantly turned from his human form back to that of leopard, and went out, and pursued, and pursued, and pursued. But, it took some time before he came in sight of the fugitives. As Horse turned to watch, he saw Leopard, his body stretched low and long in rapid leaps. Horse said to Ilâmbe, "Did I not tell you? There he is, coming!"

Horse galloped on, with foam dropping from his lips. When he saw that Leopard was gaining on them, he told Ilâmbe to take the gourd of peanuts from his back, and scatter them along behind on the ground. Leopards like peanuts, and when Ogula-Njegâ came to these nuts, he stopped to eat them. While he was eating, Horse gained time to get ahead. As soon as Leopard had finished the nuts, he started on in pursuit again, and soon began to overtake. When he approached, Horse told Ilâmbe to throw out

157

the gourd-seeds. She did so. Leopard delayed to eat these seeds also. This gave Horse time to again get ahead. Thus they went on.

Leopard, having finished the gourd-seeds, again went leaping in pursuit, and, for the third time, came near. Horse told Ilâmbe to throw the gourd of water behind, with force so that it might crash and break on the ground. As soon as she had done so, the water was turned to a stream of a deep wide river, between them and Leopard.

Then Leopard was at a loss. So, he shouted, "Ah! Ilâmbe! Mi asaiya! If I only had a chance to catch you!" But he had to turn back.

Then Horse said, "We do not know what he may do yet. Perhaps he may go around and across ahead of us. As there is a town which I know near here, we had better stay there a day or two while he may be searching for us." He added to her, "Mind! This town where we are going, well, no woman is allowed to be there, only men. So, I will change your face and dress like a man's. Be very careful how you behave when you take your bath, lest you die."

Ilâmbe promised and Horse changed her appearance. So, a fine-looking young man was seen riding into the street of the village. There were exclamations in the street, "This is a stranger! Hail! Stranger, hail! Who showed you the way to come here?"

This young man answered, "Myself. I was out riding. I saw an open path and I came in." He entered a house, and was welcomed, and they told him their times of eating, and of play. But, on the second day, as this young man went out privately, one of the men observed, and said to the other, "He acts like a woman!"

The others asked, "Really! Do you think so?"

He asserted, "Yes! I am sure!"

So, that day Ilâmbe was to meet with some trouble, for, to prove her, the men had said to her, "Tomorrow we all go bathing in the river, and you shall go with us."

She went to ask Horse what she should do. He rebuked her, "I warned you, and you have not been careful. But, do not be troubled. I will change you into a man."

That night, Ilâmbe went to Horse and he changed her. He also told her, "I warn you again. Tomorrow you go to bathe with the others, and you may take off your clothes, for, you are now a man. But, it is only for a short time, because we stay here only a day and a night more, and then we must go."

The next morning all the town went to play, and after that to bathe. When they went into the water, the other men were all expecting to see a woman revealed, but they saw that their visitor was a man. They admired his wonderfully fine physique. On emerging from the water, the men said to the one who had informed on Ilâmbe, "Did you not tell us that this was a woman? See, how great a man he is!"

As soon as they said that, the young man Ilâmbe was vexed with him, and began to berate him, saying, "Eh! You said I was a woman?" And she chased him and struck him. Then they all went back to the town.

In the evening, Horse told Ilâmbe, "I tell you what to do tomorrow. In the morning, you take your gun, and shoot me dead. After you have shot me, these men will find fault with you, saying 'Ah! You shoot your horse, and did not care for it?' But, do not say anything in reply. Cut me in pieces, and burn the pieces in the fire. After this, carefully gather all the black ashes and, very early on the following morning, in the dark before any one is up, go out of the village gateway, scatter the ashes, and you will see what will happen."

The young man did all this. On scattering the ashes, he instantly found himself changed again to a woman, and sitting on Horse's back, and they were running rapidly away.

That same day, in the afternoon, they came to the town of the father Ra-Mborakinda. On their arrival there, they told their whole story. Ilâmbe was somewhat ashamed of herself, for, she had brought these troubles on herself by insisting on having a husband with a perfectly fine skin.

So, her father said, "Ilâmbe, my child, you see the trouble you have brought on yourself. For you, a woman, to make such a demand was too much. Had I not sent Kabala with you, what would have become of you?"

The people gave Ilâmbe a glad welcome. And she went to her house, and said nothing more about fine skins.

HOW A HUNTER OBTAINED MONEY FROM HIS FRIENDS

This story has been edited and adapted from Elphinstone Dayrell's Folk Stories From Southern Nigeria, first published in 1910 by Longmans, Green And Company, London And New York.

Many years ago there was a Calabar hunter called Effiong, who lived in the bush, killed plenty of animals, and made much money. Everyone in the country knew him, and one of his best friends was a man called Okun, who lived near him. But Effiong was very extravagant, and spent much money in eating and drinking with every one, until at last he became quite poor, so he had to go out hunting again. Now his good luck seemed to have deserted him, for although he worked hard, and hunted day and night, he could not succeed in killing anything. One day, as he was very hungry, he went to his friend Okun and borrowed two hundred rods from him, and told him to come to his house on a certain day to get his money, and he told him to bring a loaded gun with him.

Now, some time before this Effiong had made friends with a leopard and a bush cat, whom he had met in the forest whilst on one of his hunting expeditions, and he had also made friends with a goat and a cock at a farm where he had stayed for the night. But though Effiong had borrowed the money from Okun, he could not think how he was to repay it on the day he had promised. At last, however, he thought of a plan, and on the next day he went to his friend the leopard, and asked him to lend him two hundred rods, promising to return the amount to him on the same day as he had promised to pay Okun, and he also told the leopard that if he were absent when he came for his money, he could kill anything he saw in the house and eat it. The leopard was then to wait until the hunter arrived, when he would pay him the money, and to this the leopard agreed.

The hunter then went to his friend the goat, and borrowed two hundred rods from him in the same way. Effiong also went to his friends the bush cat and the cock, and borrowed two hundred rods from each of them on the same conditions, and told each one of them that if he were absent when they arrived, they could kill and eat anything they found about the place.

When the appointed day arrived the hunter spread some corn on the ground, and then went away and left the house deserted. Very early in the morning, soon after he had begun to crow, the cock remembered what the hunter had told him, and walked over to the hunter's house, but found no one there. On looking round, however, he saw some corn on the ground, and, being hungry, he commenced to eat.

About this time the bush cat also arrived, and not finding the hunter at home, he, too, looked about, and very soon he spied the cock, who was busy picking up the grains of corn. So the bush cat went up very softly behind and pounced on the cock and killed him at once, and began to eat him.

By this time the goat had come for his money, but not finding his friend, he walked about until he came upon the bush cat, who was so intent upon his meal off the cock, that he did not notice the goat approaching, and the goat, being in rather a bad temper at not getting his money, at once charged at the bush cat and knocked him over, butting him with his horns. This the bush cat did not like at all, so, as he was not big enough to fight the goat, he picked up the remains of the cock and ran off with it to the bush, and so lost his money, as he did not await the arrival of the hunter.

The goat was thus left master of the situation and started bleating, and this noise attracted the attention of the leopard, who was on his way to receive payment from the hunter. As he got nearer the smell of goat became very strong, and being hungry, for he had not eaten anything for some time, the leopard approached the goat very carefully. Not seeing any one about he stalked the goat and got nearer and nearer, until he was within springing distance. The goat, in the meantime, was grazing quietly, quite unsuspicious of any danger, as he was in his friend the hunter's compound. Now and then he would say Ba!! But most of the time he was busy eating the young grass, and picking up the leaves which had fallen from a tree of which he was very fond. Suddenly the leopard sprang at the goat, and with one crunch at the neck brought him down. The goat was dead almost at once, and the leopard started on his meal.

It was now about eight o'clock in the morning, and Okun, the hunter's friend, having had his early morning meal, went out with his gun to receive payment of the two hundred rods he had lent to the hunter. When he got close to the house he heard a crunching sound, and, being a hunter himself, he approached very cautiously, and looking over the fence saw the leopard only a few yards off busily engaged eating the goat. He took careful aim at the leopard and fired, whereupon the leopard rolled over dead.

The death of the leopard meant that four of the hunter's creditors were now disposed of, as the bush cat had killed the cock, the goat had driven the bush cat away so that he thus forfeited his claim, and in his turn the goat had been killed by the leopard, who had just been slain by Okun. This meant a saving of eight hundred rods to Effiong, but he was not content with this, and directly he heard the report of the gun he ran out from where he had been hiding all the time, and found the leopard lying dead with Okun standing over it.

Then in very strong language Effiong began to upbraid his friend, and asked him why he had killed his old friend the leopard, that nothing would satisfy him but that he should report the whole matter to the king, who would no doubt deal with him as he thought fit. When Effiong said this Okun was frightened, and begged him not to say anything more about the matter, as the king would be angry, but the hunter was obdurate, and refused to listen to him, and at last Okun said, "If you will allow the whole thing to drop and will say no more about it, I will make you a present of the two hundred rods you borrowed from me."

This was just what Effiong wanted, but still he did not give in at once, but eventually he agreed, and told Okun he might go, and that he would bury the body of his friend the leopard.

Directly Okun had gone, instead of burying the body Effiong dragged it inside the house and skinned it very carefully. The skin he put out to dry in the sun, and covered it with wood ash, and the body he ate. When the skin was well cured the hunter took it to a distant market, where he sold it for much money.

And now, whenever a bush cat sees a cock he always kills it, and does so by right, as he takes the cock in part payment of the two hundred rods which the hunter never paid him.

The moral of this goes like this: never lend money to people, because if they cannot pay they will try to kill you or get rid of you in some way, either by poison or by setting bad Ju-Ju's for you.

ORIGIN OF THE ELEPHANT

This story has been edited and adapted from Robert Hamill Nassau's Where Animals Talk, first published in 1912 by Richard G. Badger at The Gorham Press, based out of Boston. This tale was originally told by storytellers from the Benga tribe.

Uhâdwe, Bokume, and Njâku were human beings, all three born of one mother. As time went on, Uhâdwe called his brethren, Bokume and Njâku, and said, "My brothers! Let us separate. I am going to the Great Sea. You, Bokume go to the Forest, while you, Njâku, also go to the Forest."

Bokume went to the forest and grew up there, and became the valuable mahogany tree (Okume).

Njâku departed, but he went in anger, saying, "I will not remain in the forest, I am going to build with the towns-people."

He came striding back to the town. As he emerged there from the forest, his feet swelled and swelled, and became elephant feet. His ear extended way down. His teeth spread and one of them grew to become a tusk, and then another one grew to become a tusk. The towns-people began to hoot at him. And he turned back to the forest. But, as he went, he said to them, "In my going now to the Forest, I and whatever plants you shall plant in the forest shall journey together. I will destroy all of your crops!"

When Uhâdwe arrived at the sea he saw there a stem of bush-rope, the Calamus palm, and the staff he held turned into a mangrove forest. The footprints where he and his dog trod are there on the beach of Corisco Bay until this day. He created a sand-bank where he stood, extending through the ocean, by which he crossed over to the Land of the Great Sea. When he reached that Land, he prepared a ship. He put into it every production by which white people obtain wealth, and he said to the crew, "Go and take for me my brother."

The ship came to Africa and put down anchor, but, for four days the crew did not find any person coming from shore to set foot on the ship, or to go from the ship to set foot ashore, the natives being destitute of canoes.

Finally, Uhâdwe came and appeared to the towns-people in a dream, and said, "Go to the forest and cut down Njâpe, dig out a canoe, and go alongside the ship."

Early next morning they went to the forest, and came to the Okume trees where they cut one down and hacked it into shape. They launched it on the sea, and said to their young men, "Go!"

Four young men went into the canoe to go alongside the ship. When they had nearly reached it, looking here and there they became frightened, and they stopped paddling. The white men on the ship made repeated signs to them. Then the young men, having come close, spoke to the white men in the native language. A white man answered also in the same language. That white man said, "I have come to buy the tusks of the beast which is here in the forest with big feet and tusks and great ears. The beast is called Njâku."

They said, "Yes! A good thing!"

Before they left the white gave them four bunches of tobacco, four bales of prints, four caps, and some other things. When they reached the shore, they told the others, "The white men want Njâku's tusks, and also they have things we can use to to kill his tribe."

The next morning, they went to the white men. The white men gave them guns and bullets and powder. They went to the forest, and fought with the elephants. In two days the ship was loaded, and it departed.

This continued to happen for many, many years in the Ivory-Trade and still continues unlawfully to this day.

OF THE PRETTY GIRL AND THE SEVEN JEALOUS WOMEN

This story has been edited and adapted from Elphinstone Dayrell's Folk Stories From Southern Nigeria, first published in 1910 by Longmans, Green And Company, London And New York.

There was once a very beautiful girl called Akim. She was a native of Ibibio, and the name was given to her on account of her good looks, as she was born in the spring-time. She was an only daughter, and her parents were extremely fond of her. The people of the town, and more particularly the young girls, were so jealous of Akim's good looks and beautiful form, for she was perfectly made, very strong, and her carriage, bearing, and manners were most graceful, that her parents would not allow her to join the young girls' society in the town, as is customary for all young people to do, both boys and girls belonging to a company according to their age. These companies consisted, as a rule, of all the boys or girls born in the same year.

Akim's parents were rather poor, but she was a good daughter, and gave them no trouble, so they had a happy home. One day as Akim was on her way to draw water from the spring she met the company of seven girls, to which in an ordinary way she would have belonged, if her parents had not forbidden her. These girls told her that they were going to hold a play in the town in three days' time, and asked her to join them. She said she was very sorry, but that her parents were poor, and only had herself to work for them, and she had no time to spare for dancing and plays. She then left them and went home.

In the evening the seven girls met together, and as they were very envious of Akim, they discussed how they should be revenged upon her for refusing to join their company, and they talked for a long time as to how they could get Akim into danger or punish her in some way.

At last one of the girls suggested that they should all go to Akim's house every day and help her with her work, so that when they had made friends with her they would be able to entice her away and take their revenge upon her for being more beautiful than themselves. Although they went every day and helped Akim and her parents with their work, the parents knew that they were jealous of their daughter, and repeatedly warned her not on any account to go with them, as they were not to be trusted.

At the end of the year there was going to be a big play, called the new yam play, to which Akim's parents had been invited. The play was going to be held at a town about two hours' march from where they lived. Akim was very anxious to go and take part in the dance, but her parents gave her plenty of work to do before they started, thinking that this would surely prevent her going, as she was a very obedient daughter, and always did her work properly.

On the morning of the play the jealous seven came to Akim and asked her to go with them, but she pointed to all the water-pots she had to fill, and showed them where her parents had told her to polish the walls with a stone and make the floor good, and after that was finished she had to pull up all the weeds round the house and clean up all round. She therefore said it was impossible for her to leave the house until all the work was finished. When the girls heard this they took up the water-pots, went to the spring, and quickly returned with them full. They placed them in a row, and then they got stones, and very soon had the walls polished and the floor made good. After that they did the weeding outside and the cleaning up, and when everything was completed they said to Akim, "Now then, come along. You have no excuse to remain behind, as all the work is done."

Akim really wanted to go to the play, so as all the work was done which her parents had told her to do, she finally consented to go. About half-way to the town, where the new yam play was being held, there was a small river, about five feet deep, which had to be crossed by wading, as there was no bridge. In this river there was a powerful Ju-Ju, whose law was that whenever anyone crossed the river and returned the same way on the return journey, whoever it was, had to give some food to the Ju-Ju. If they did not make the proper sacrifice the Ju-Ju dragged them down and took them to his home, and kept them there to work for him. The seven jealous girls knew all about this Ju-Ju, having often crossed the river before, as they walked about all over the country, and had plenty of friends in the different towns. Akim, however, who was a good girl, and never went anywhere, knew nothing about this Ju-Ju, which her companions had found out.

When the work was finished they all started off together, and crossed the river without any trouble. When they had gone a small distance on the other side they saw a small bird, perched on a high tree, who admired Akim very much, and sang in praise of her beauty, much to the annoyance of the seven girls, but they walked on without saying anything, and eventually arrived at the town where the play was being held. Akim had not taken the trouble to change her clothes, but when she arrived at the town, although her companions had on all their best beads and their finest clothes, the young men and people admired Akim far more than the other girls, and she was declared to be the finest and most beautiful woman at the dance. They gave her plenty of palm wine, foo-foo, and everything she wanted, so that the seven girls became more angry and jealous than before.

The people danced and sang all that night, but Akim managed to keep out of the sight of her parents until the following morning, when they asked her how it was that she had disobeyed them and neglected her work. Akim told them that the work had all been done by her friends, and they had enticed her to come to the play with them. Her mother then told her to return home at once, and that she was not to remain in the town any longer.

When Akim told her friends this they said, "Very well, we are just going to have some small meal, and then we will return with you."

They all then sat down together and had their food, but each of the seven jealous girls hid a small quantity of foo-foo and fish in her clothes for the Water Ju-Ju. However Akim, who knew nothing about this, as her parents had forgotten to tell her about the Ju-Ju, never thinking for one moment that their daughter would cross the river, did not take any food with her as a sacrifice to the Ju-Ju.

When they arrived at the river Akim saw the girls making their small sacrifices, and begged them to give her a small share so that she could do the same, but they refused, and all walked across the river safely. Then when it was Akim's turn to cross, when she arrived in the middle of the river, the Water Ju-Ju caught hold of her and dragged her underneath the water, so that she immediately disappeared from sight. The seven girls had been watching for this, and when they saw that she had gone they went on their way, very pleased at the success of their scheme, and said to one another, "Now Akim is gone for ever, and we shall hear no more about her being better-looking than we are."

As there was no one to be seen at the time when Akim disappeared they naturally thought that their cruel action had escaped detection, so they went home rejoicing, but they never noticed the little bird high up in the tree who had sung of Akim's beauty when they were on their way to the play. The little bird was very sorry for Akim, and made up his mind that, when the proper time came, he would tell her parents what he had seen, so that perhaps they would be able to save her. The bird had heard Akim asking for a small portion of the food to make a sacrifice with, and had heard all the girls refusing to give her any.

The following morning, when Akim's parents returned home, they were much surprised to find that the door was fastened, and that there was no sign of their daughter anywhere about the place, so they inquired of their neighbours, but no one was able to give them any information about her. They then went to the seven girls, and asked them what had become of Akim. They replied that they did not know what had become of her, but that she had reached their town safely with them, and then said she was going home.

The father then went to his Ju-Ju man, who, by casting lots, discovered what had happened, and told him that on her way back from the play Akim had crossed the river without making the customary sacrifice to the Water Ju-Ju, and that, as the Ju-Ju was angry, he had seized Akim and taken her to his home. He therefore told Akim's father to take one goat, one basketful of eggs, and one piece of white cloth to the river in the morning, and to offer them as a sacrifice to the Water Ju-Ju. Then Akim would be thrown out of the water seven times, but that if her father failed to catch her on the seventh time, she would disappear for ever.

Akim's father then returned home, and, when he arrived there, the little bird who had seen Akim taken by the Water Ju-Ju, told him everything that had happened, confirming the Ju-Ju's words. He also said that it was entirely the fault of the seven girls, who had refused to give Akim any food to make the sacrifice with.

Early the following morning the parents went to the river, and made the sacrifice as advised by the Ju-Ju. Immediately they had done so, the Water Ju-Ju threw Akim up from the middle of the river. Her father caught her at once, and returned home very thankfully.

He never told anyone, however, that he had recovered his daughter, but made up his mind to punish the seven jealous girls, so he dug a deep pit in the middle of his house, and placed dried palm leaves and sharp stakes in the bottom of the pit. He then covered the top of the pit with new mats, and sent out word for all people to come and hold a play to rejoice with him, as he had recovered his daughter from the spirit land. Many people came, and danced and sang all the day and night, but the seven jealous girls did not appear, as they were frightened. However, as they were told that everything had gone well on the previous day, and that there had been no trouble, they went to the house the following morning and mixed with the dancers, but they were ashamed to look Akim in the face, who was sitting down in the middle of the dancing ring.

When Akim's father saw the seven girls he pretended to welcome them as his daughter's friends, and presented each of them with a brass rod, which he placed round their necks. He also gave them tombo to drink. He then picked them out, and told them to go and sit on mats on the other side of the pit he had prepared for them. When they walked over the mats which hid the pit they all fell in, and Akim's father immediately got some red-hot ashes from the fire and threw them in on top of the screaming girls, who were in great pain. At once the dried palm leaves caught fire, killing all the girls at once. When the people heard the cries and saw the smoke, they all ran back to the town.

The next day the parents of the dead girls went to the head chief, and complained that Akim's father had killed their daughters, so the chief called him before him, and asked him for an explanation. Akim's father went at once to the chief, taking the Ju-Ju man, whom everybody relied upon, and the small bird, as his witnesses.

When the chief had heard the whole case, he told Akim's father that he should only have killed one girl to avenge his daughter, and not seven. So he told the father to bring Akim before him. When she arrived, the head chief, seeing how beautiful she was, said that her father was justified in killing all the seven girls on her behalf, so he dismissed the case, and told the parents of the dead girls to go away and mourn for their daughters, who had been wicked and jealous women, and had been properly punished for their cruel behaviour to Akim.

The moral of this story is that you should never kill a man or a woman because you are envious of their beauty, as if you do, you will surely be punished.

HOW DISEASES WERE BROUGHT TO THE TRIBE

This story has been edited and adapted from Captain R. S. Rattray's Akan-Ashanti Folk-Tales, first published in 1930 by Oxford University Press – American Branch, New York.

Anansi went to the Sky-God Nyame one day. He wanted to take one of Nyame's sheep, named Kra Kwame, and eat it. Anansi told Nyame that if he was allowed, he would bring Nyame a maiden as a gift from one of the villages in return. Nyame agreed and gave him the sheep, so Anansi left and set out for his home, later preparing the sheep. Once he was finished preparing it, Anansi searched for a village and discovered one where only women lived. The Spider settled there and gave each of them some of the sheep he had killed, marrying every woman in the village and forsaking his promise to Nyame. Soon however, a hunter visited the village that Anansi had settled in and witnessed what he was doing.

The hunter soon left and went to Nyame, reporting what he'd seen in the village. Nyame became furious upon learning of Anansi's deception and ordered his messengers to go the village Anansi was living in and take every woman there. His messengers obeyed and took every woman, save one that was ill at that time, and presented them to Nyame. Disappointed, Anansi wasn't sure what he'd do as he now only had one remaining wife, and she was too sick to help him. He asked her and she simply told Anansi to gather a gourd and bathe her, filling up the gourd with the water he'd used afterward. That water would then house all of the diseases that had afflicted her. Anansi obeyed his wife and she became incredibly beautiful. Anansi realized she was more beautiful than any of the other wives he'd taken on while living in the tribe, in fact, and smitten by her, Anansi remarried the woman. Yet, the hunter visited the village again. He saw Anansi's wife, now beautiful beyond comparison, and returned to Nyame to report what he'd discovered.

The hunter told Nyame that Anansi had tricked him, because the women that Nyame had taken from Anansi were all hideous in comparison to the beautiful woman Anansi had as his current wife. Nyame was furious again. He ordered his messengers to send for her, and they went to Anansi's village looking for the woman. Anansi met them and they told him of Nyame's wish. He complied, showed them where his wife was, and they took her with them to Nyame. Anansi however, had a plan of his own, and began his scheme once they left.

Anansi searched for the gourd that had the water he'd bathed his wife with, and then took a skin and made a drum with it. He then made another drum and called for his son Ntikuma. Together the two began beating the drums and dancing while singing vulgarities. Anene the crow, another messenger of Nyame, saw what Anansi was doing and told Nyame about the dance. Nyame then sent his messengers and asked them to bring Anansi to him, as he wanted the Spider to perform the dance for him. Anansi however, told them that he could only perform his dance around his wives and that he needed his drum. He promised that he would dance before Nyame if he agreed to this, so the messengers informed Nyame and he agreed to Anansi's terms. The messengers then brought Anansi to the harem where his wives were kept and he began playing. Soon Nyame came and danced to the song while the former wives of Anansi joined in.

Anansi's final wife however, recognized the gourd Anansi's drum was made from and decided not to dance, suspecting Anansi's trickery. Yet, she was coerced into joining Nyame in the performance. Before she could begin however, Anansi opened the drum and tossed all the water from the gourd on the ground. All of the diseases that had once washed away now returned and sickness fell upon the tribe. So it was that the Sky God caused Anansi to bring all illnesses to the world.

WHY GOATS BECAME DOMESTIC

This story has been edited and adapted from Robert Hamill Nassau's Where Animals Talk, first published in 1912 by Richard G. Badger at The Gorham Press, based out of Boston. This tale was originally told by storytellers from the Benga tribe.

Goat and his mother lived alone in their village. He said to her, "I have here a magic-medicine to strengthen one in wrestling. There is no one who can overcome me, or cast me down. I can overcome any other person."

The other Beasts heard of this boast, and they took up the challenge. First, House-Rats, hundreds of them, came to Goat's village, to test him. And they began the wrestling. He overcame them, one by one, to the number of two hundred. So, the Rats went back to their places, admitting that they were not able to overcome him.

Then, Forest-Rats came to wrestle with Goat. He overcame them also, all of them. And they went back to their own place defeated.

Then, the Antelope came to wrestle with Goat. He overcame all the Antelopes, every one of them. Not one was able to withstand him. And they also went back to their places.

Also, Elephant with all the elephants, came on that same challenge. Goat overcame all the Elephants, and they too, went back to their place.

Thus, all the Beasts came, in the same way, and were overcome in the same way, and went back in the same way.

But, there still remained one Beast, Leopard, who had not made the attempt. So he said he would go, as he was sure he could overcome Goat. He came. Goat overcame him also. So, it was proved that not a single beast could withstand Goat.

Then the Father of All-the-Leopards said, "I am ashamed that this Beast should overcome me. I will kill him!"

He made a plan to do so. He went to the spring where Mankind got their drinking-water. He stood, hiding at the spring. Men of the town went to the spring to get water, and Leopard killed two of them. The people went to tell Goat, "Go away from here, for Leopard is killing Mankind on your account."

The Mother of Goat said to him, "If that is so, let us go to my brother Vyâdu."

So they both went to go to Uncle Antelope. And they came to his village. When they told him their errand, he bravely said, "Remain here! Let me see Njâ come here with his audacity!"

They were then at Antelope's village, about two days. On the third day, about eight o'clock in the morning, Leopard came there as if for a walk. When Antelope saw him, Goat and his mother hid themselves, and Antelope asked Leopard, "What is your anger? Why are you angry with my nephew?"

At that very moment while Antelope was speaking, Leopard seized him on the ear. Antelope cried out, "What are you killing me for?"

Leopard replied, "Show me the place where Tomba-Taba and his mother are."

So, Antelope being afraid said, "Come tonight, and I will show you where they sleep. And you kill them, but don't kill me."

While he was saying this, Goat overheard, and said to his mother, "We must flee, lest Njâ kill us."

So, at sun-down, that evening, Goat and his mother fled to the village of Elephant. About midnight, Leopard came to Antelope's village, according to appointment, and looked for Goat, but did not find him. Leopard went to all the houses of the village, and when he came to Antelope's own, in his disappointment, he killed him.

Leopard kept up his search, and followed to find where Goat had gone. Following the tracks, he came to the village of Elephant. When he arrived there, Elephant demanded, "What's the matter?"

And the same conversation was held, as at Antelope's village, and the incidents happened as at that village, ending with Elephant being killed by Leopard. Goat and his mother had fled, and had gone to the village of Ox.

Leopard followed, and came to Ox's village. There all the same things were said and done, ending with Goat and his mother fleeing, and Ox being killed.

Then, the mother, wearying of flight, and sorry at causing their hosts to be killed, said, "My child! If we continue to flee to the villages of other beasts, Njâ will follow, and will kill them. Let us flee to the homes of Mankind."

So, they fled again, and came to the town of Man, and told him their story. He received them kindly. He took Goat and his mother as guests, and gave them a house to live in.

One time, at night, Leopard came to the town of Man, in pursuit of Goat. But Man said to Leopard, "Those Beasts whom you killed, failed to find a way in which to kill you. But, if you come here, we will find a way."

So, that night, Leopard went back to his village.

On another day, Mankind began to make a big trap, with two rooms in it. They took Goat and put him in one room of the trap. Night came. Leopard left his village, still going to seek for Goat, and he came again to the town of Man. Leopard stood still, listened, and sniffed the air. He smelled the odor of Goat, and was glad, and said, "So! This night I will kill him!"

He saw an open way to a small house. He thought it was a door. He entered, and was caught in the trap. He could see Goat through the cracks in the wall, but could not get at him. Goat jeered at him, "My friend! You were about to kill me, but you are unable."

Daybreak came. And people of Man's town found Leopard in the trap, caught fast. They took machetes and guns, and killed him. Then Man said to Goat, "You shall not go back to the Forest. You will remain here always."

This is the reason that Goats like to live with mankind, through fear of Leopards.

THE 'NSASAK BIRD AND THE ODUDU BIRD

This story has been edited and adapted from Elphinstone Dayrell's Folk Stories From Southern Nigeria, first published in 1910 by Longmans, Green And Company, London And New York.

A long time ago, in the days of King Adam of Calabar, the king wanted to know if there was any animal or bird which was capable of enduring hunger for a long period. When he found one the king said he would make him a chief of his tribe.

The 'Nsasak bird is very small, having a shining breast of green and red. He also has blue and yellow feathers and red round the neck, and his chief food consists of ripe palm nuts. The Odudu bird, on the other hand, is much larger, about the size of a magpie, with plenty of feathers, but a very thin body. He has a long tail, and his colouring is black and brown with a cream-coloured breast. He lives chiefly on grasshoppers, and is also very fond of crickets, which make a noise at night.

Both the 'Nsasak bird and the Odudu were great friends, and used to live together. They both made up their minds that they would go before the king and try to be made chiefs, but the Odudu bird was quite confident that he would win, as he was so much bigger than the 'Nsasak bird. He therefore offered to starve for seven days.

The king then told them both to build houses which he would inspect, and then he would have them fastened up, and the one who could remain the longest without eating would be made the chief.

They both then built their houses, but the 'Nsasak bird, who was very cunning, thought that he could not possibly live for seven days without eating anything. He therefore made a tiny hole in the wall, being very small himself, which he covered up so that the king would not notice it on his inspection. The king then came and looked carefully over both houses, but failed to detect the little hole in the 'Nsasak bird's house, as it had been hidden so carefully. He therefore declared that both houses were safe, and then ordered the two birds to go inside their respective houses, and the doors were carefully fastened on the outside.

Every morning at dawn the 'Nsasak bird used to escape through the small opening he had left high up in the wall, and fly away a long distance and enjoy himself all day, taking care, however, that none of the people on the farms should see him. Then when the sun went down he would fly back to his little house and creep through the hole in the wall, closing it carefully after him. When he was safely inside he would call out to his friend the Odudu and ask him if he felt hungry, and told him that he must bear it well if he wanted to win, as he, the 'Nsasak bird, was very fit, and could go on for a long time.

For several days this went on, the voice of the Odudu bird growing weaker and weaker every night, until at last he could no longer reply. Then the little bird knew that his friend must be dead. He was very sorry, but could not report the matter, as he was supposed to be confined inside his house.

When the seven days had expired the king came and had both the doors of the houses opened. The 'Nsasak bird at once flew out, and, perching on a branch of a tree which grew near, sang most merrily, but the Odudu bird was found to be quite dead, and there was very little left of him, as the ants had eaten most of his body, leaving only the feathers and bones on the floor.

The king therefore at once appointed the 'Nsasak bird to be the head chief of all the small birds, and in the Ibibio country even to the present time the small boys who have bows and arrows are presented with a prize, which sometimes takes the shape of a female goat, if they manage to shoot a 'Nsasak bird, as the 'Nsasak bird is the king of the small birds, and most difficult to shoot on account of his wiliness and his small size.

DOG, AND HIS HUMAN SPEECH

This story has been edited and adapted from Robert Hamill Nassau's Where Animals Talk, first published in 1912 by Richard G. Badger at The Gorham Press, based out of Boston. This tale was originally told by storytellers from the Benga tribe.

Dog and his mother were the only inhabitants of their hamlet. He had the power to speak both as a beast and as a human being.

One day the mother said to the son, "You are now a strong man. Go, and seek a marriage. Go, and marry Eyâle, the daughter of Njambo."

And he said to his mother, "I will go tomorrow."

That day darkened. And they both went to lie down in their places for sleep. Then soon, another day began to break.

Dog said to his mother, "This is the time of my journey."

It was about sun-rise in the morning. And he began his journey. He went the distance of about eight miles, and arrived at the journey's end before the middle of the morning.

He entered the house of Njambo, the father of Eyâle. Njambo and his wife saluted him, "Mbolo!" and he responded, "Ai! mbolo!" Njambo asked him, "My friend! What is the cause of your journey?"

Dog, with his animal language, answered, "I have come to marry your daughter Eyâle."

Njambo consented, and the mother of the girl also agreed. They called their daughter, and asked her, and she also replied, "Yes! with all my heart." This young woman was of very fine appearance in face and body. So, all the parties agreed to the marriage.

After that, about sun-set in the evening, when they sat down at supper, the son-in-law, Dog, was not able to eat for some unknown reason. That day darkened, and they went to their sleep.

And, then, daylight broke. But, by an hour after sunrise in the morning, Dog had not risen, for he was still asleep.

The mother of the woman said to her, "Get some water ready for the washing of your husband's face, whenever he shall awake." She also said to her daughter, "I am going to go into the forest to the plantation to get food for your husband, for, since his coming, he has not eaten. Also, here is a chicken. The lads may kill and prepare it. But, you yourself must split ngândâ gourd-seeds to m and mash into a pudding."

She handed Eyâle the dish of gourd-seeds, and went off into the forest. Njambo also went away on an errand with his wife. The daughter took the dish of seeds, and, sitting down, began to shell them. As she shelled the seeds, she threw the kernels on the ground, but the shells she put on a plate.

Shortly after the mother had gone, Dog woke from sleep. He rose from his bed, and came out to the room where his wife was, and stood near her, watching her working at the seeds. He stood silent, looking closely, and observed that she was still throwing away the kernels, the good part, and saving the shells on the plate. He spoke to her with his human voice, "No! Woman! Not so! Why do you throw the good parts to the ground, and keep the worthless husks on the plate?"

While he was thus speaking to his wife, she suddenly fell to the ground. And at once she died. He laid hold of her to lift her up. But, she was a corpse.

Soon afterwards, the father and the mother came, having returned from their errands. They found their child a corpse, and they said to Dog, "Mbwa! What is this?"

He, with his own language replied, "I cannot tell."

But, they insisted, "Tell us the reason!"

So Dog spoke with his human voice, "You, Woman, went to the forest while I was asleep. You, Man, you also went in company of your wife, while I was asleep. When I rose from sleep, I found my wife was cracking ngândâ. She was taking the good kernels to throw on the ground, and was keeping the shells for the plate. And I spoke and told her, 'The good kernels which you are throwing on the ground are to be eaten, not the husks.'"

While he was telling them this, they too, also fell to the ground, and died, apparently without cause.

When the people of the town heard about all this, they said, "This person carries an evil Medicine for killing people. Let him be seized and killed!"

So Dog fled away rapidly into the forest, and he finally reached the hamlet where his mother lived. His body was scratched and torn by the branches and thorns of the bushes of the forest during his hasty flight. His mother exclaimed, "Mbwa! What's the matter? Such haste! And your body so disordered!"

He replied, using their own language, "No! I won't tell you. I won't speak."

But, his mother begged him, "Please, my child, tell me!"

So, finally, he spoke, using his strange voice, and said, "My mother! I tell you! Njambo and his wife liked me for the marriage, and the woman consented entirely. I was at that time asleep, when the Man and his wife went to the forest. When I rose from my sleep, I found the woman Eyâle cracking ngândâ, and throwing away the kernels, and keeping the husks. And I told her, 'The good ones which you are throwing away are the ones to be eaten.' And, at once she died."

While he was speaking thus to his mother, she also fell dead on the ground. The news was carried to the town of Dog's mother's brother, and very many people came to the Mourning. His Uncle came to Dog, and said, "Mbwa! What is the reason of all this?"

But Dog would not answer. He only said, "No! I won't speak." Then they all begged him, "Tell us the reason."

But he replied only, "No! I won't speak."

Finally, as they urged him, he chose two of them, and said to the company, "The rest of you remain here, and watch while I go and speak to these two."

Then Dog spoke to those two men with the same voice as he had to his mother. And, at once they died, just as she had died. Then he exclaimed, "Ah! No! If I speak so, people will come to an end!"

And all the people agreed, "Yes, Mbwa! It is so. Your human speech kills us people. Don't speak any more."

And he went away to live with Mankind but has never spoken the words of man since.

CONCERNING THE HAWK AND THE OWL

This story has been edited and adapted from Elphinstone Dayrell's Folk Stories From Southern Nigeria, first published in 1910 by Longmans, Green And Company, London And New York.

In the olden days when Effiong was king of Calabar, it was customary at that time for rulers to give big feasts, to which all the subjects and all the birds of the air and animals of the forest, also the fish and other things that lived in the water, were invited. All the people, birds, animals, and fish, were under the king, and had to obey him. His favourite messenger was the hawk, as he could travel so quickly.

The hawk served the king faithfully for several years, and when he wanted to retire, he asked what the king proposed to do for him, as very soon he would be too old to work anymore. So the king told the hawk to bring any living creature, bird or animal, to him, and he would allow the hawk for the future to live on that particular species without any trouble. The hawk then flew over a lot of country, and went from forest to forest, until at last he found a young owl which had tumbled out of its nest. This the hawk brought to the king, who told him that for the future he might eat owls. The hawk then carried the owlet away, and told his friends what the king had said.

One of the wisest of them said, "Tell me when you seized the young owlet, what did the parents say?" And the hawk replied that the father and mother owls kept quite quiet, and never said anything. The hawk's friend then advised him to return the owlet to his parents, as he could never tell what the owls would do to him in the night-time, and as they had made no noise, they were no doubt plotting in their minds some deep and cruel revenge.

The next day the hawk carried the owlet back to his parents and left him near the nest. He then flew about, trying to find some other bird which would do as his food, but as all the birds had heard that the hawk had seized the owlet, they hid themselves, and would not come out when the hawk was near. He therefore could not catch any birds.

As he was flying home he saw a lot of fowls near a house, basking in the sun and scratching in the dust. There were also several small chickens running about and chasing insects, or picking up anything they could find to eat, with the old hen following them and clucking and calling to them from time to time. When the hawk saw the chickens, he made up his mind that he would take one, so he swooped down and caught the smallest in his strong claws.

Immediately he had seized the chicken the cocks began to make a great noise, and the hen ran after him and tried to make him drop her child, calling loudly, with her feathers fluffed out and making dashes at him. But he carried it off, and all the fowls and chickens at once ran screaming into the houses, some taking shelter under bushes and others trying to hide themselves in the long grass. He then carried the chicken to the king, telling him that he had returned the owlet to his parents, as he did not want him for food; so the king told the hawk that for the future he could always feed on chickens.

The hawk then took the chicken home, and his friend who dropped in to see him, asked him what the parents of the chicken had done when they saw their child taken away.

The hawk said, "They all made a lot of noise, and the old hen chased me, but although there was a great disturbance amongst the fowls, nothing happened."

His friend then said as the fowls had made much palaver, he was quite safe to kill and eat the chickens, as the people who made plenty of noise in the daytime would go to sleep at night and not disturb him, or do him any injury. The only people to be afraid of were those who when they were injured, kept quite silent. You might be certain then that they were plotting mischief, and would do harm in the night-time.

HOW KWAKU ANANSI TOOK ASO AS HIS WIFE, AND HOW JEALOUSY CAME TO THE TRIBE

This story has been edited and adapted from Captain R. S. Rattray's Akan-Ashanti Folk-Tales, first published in 1930 by Oxford University Press – American Branch, New York.

A long time ago, Aso was not yet married to Anansi. Instead, she was married to another man, known as Akwasi-the-jealous-one. Befitting his name, he was very possessive of Aso and wanted no one else to see or interact with her, so he built a small village where only the two of them lived. Akwasi-the-jealous-one was especially worried about losing Aso because he was sterile and knew that others would take her away from him if he and Aso lived among other people.

One day, Nyame grew tired of Akwasi-the-jealous-one's failure and told young men in the other villages about his marriage with Aso. Nyame told the men that the first man to take Aso from Akwasi-the-jealous-one and sire a child with her could marry her. However, all of the men who accepted his challenge failed to capture Aso. Anansi watched all that transpired and soon went to Nyame himself. He promised Nyame that he could accomplish what other men had not. The Sky-God asked if Anansi was certain and the Spider answered that he would be able to as long as he was given the items he requested to help him, namely medicine to make guns as well as bullets. Nyame accepted his request and gave Anansi what he needed.

Anansi then went to many villages and told them that Nyame had told him to bring the powder and bullets to them so that they could go hunting for him. Anansi told them that he would return and then take the meat they collected so that he could give it to Nyame. They agreed to his request and he then distributed powder and bullets amongst them until all villages had some. Anansi then left for a time and wove a palm-leaf basket, returning when he had finished to the villages he'd distributed hunting supplies to. In turn, he received all they'd hunted and soon headed for Akwasi-the-jealous-one's settlement.

Eventually, Anansi came upon a river where Akwasi and Aso drank. He took some of the meat and placed it into the water. He then carried the basket with him, which still had more than enough meat in it, and reached Akwasi-the-jealous-one's village. Aso noticed Anansi arrive and called out to her husband, surprised that Anansi had come. Kwasi-the-jealous-one came out and inquired who Anansi was, and the Spider replied that he'd come by the order of Nyame and he wanted to rest on his journey. Akwasi-the-jealous-one welcomed Anansi to his village.

Aso noticed the meat Anansi had left in the river and told him what she'd discovered. Anansi simply replied that she was welcome to have it as he didn't need it, and he then informed Aso that she could feed any pets they possessed with it. Aso collected it, offering the meat to her husband. Anansi then asked Aso to cook him some food, and she obliged, preparing to make Fufu.

Soon, Aso began preparing Fufu for Anansi, but he told her it was not enough when he learned what she was making. Anansi then asked her to use a larger pot, and when Aso did so, Anansi offered more of the meat he'd collected, with one caveat. Out of the meat he possessed, Aso could only cook the thighs, which numbered some forty pieces. Aso agreed and she then placed the food alongside the rest she'd prepared when she finished cooking it. Aso then collected her own portion and everyone began eating.

Anansi, however, was not satisfied and complained, saying that the fufu Aso had prepared lacked salt. Akwasi-the-jealous-one then asked Aso to bring some salt for Anansi, but the Spider objected. He told Akwasi that it was rude to command her to gather the salt when she was eating and suggested that Akwasi should get the salt instead. Akwasi-the-jealous-one accepted Anansi's advice and left to find more salt, while Anansi secretly snuck medicine from his pouch and put it into Akwasi's fufu.

Akwasi-the-jealous-one soon returned, but Anansi informed Aso's husband that he was full and no longer needed any more food. Akwasi set the salt aside and began eating his fufu again, completely oblivious to what Anansi had done.

Eventually, Akwasi-the-jealous-one realized he did not know Anansi's name, and asked the Spider what he was called. Anansi replied that his name was "Rise-up-and-make-love-to-Aso," which startled Akwasi, so he asked his wife Aso if she'd heard his name as well. Aso acknowledged that she did. Akwasi then left to prepare a room for Anansi.

When Akwasi finished, he told Anansi to sleep there, but Anansi replied that he couldn't, because he was Nyame's Soul-washer and only slept in a room with an open veranda. His parents had also conceived him in the open, so he was forbidden from sleeping in closed rooms.

Akwasi-the-jealous-one then asked Anansi where he wished to sleep instead, but Anansi then made another excuse. The open room had to be in a house that belonged to Nyame. To do otherwise would make Akwasi equal to Nyame and break the commandment Anansi'd been given. Thus, Anansi asked Akwasi-the-jealous-one to give him a sleeping mat so he could sleep in front of their room while they slept.

Soon, Anansi laid upon the sleeping mat and waited for Akwasi and his wife Aso to fall sleep. He sang a song to the gods while he played his sepirewa, certain the plan he'd concocted would be successful.

"Akuamoa Ananse, we shall achieve something today.

Ananse, the child of Nsia, the mother of Nyame, the Sky-god,

Today we shall achieve something, today.

Ananse, the Soul-washer to the Nyame, the Sky-god,

Today, I shall see something."

Once Anansi finished, he put his sepirewa aside and fell asleep.

Suddenly, Anansi awoke because he could hear Akwasi-the-jealous-one calling out to him. Akwasi, however, refused to call the Spider by the made up name that he had given to Akwasi, so Anansi remained silent. The medicine that Anansi had poisoned Akwasi-the-jealous-one with had worked. Akwasi tried another time, but refused to call Anansi by the name he'd given him again, so Anansi did not answer him. Eventually, Akwasi succumbed and finally pleaded "Rise-up-and-make-love-to-Aso," falling for Anansi's scheme. Anansi responded to Akwasi-the-jealous-one and opened his door, asking Akwasi what troubled him. Akwasi said that he needed to leave for a moment, and then left.

Once Akwasi-the-jealous-one was gone, the Spider went into the man's room and saw that Aso was awake. Anansi asked her if she'd heard what Akwasi had said, but she had not and she instead asked Anansi to tell her. Anansi repeated the name he'd given to them, implying that he was to make love to her. Aso accepted Anansi's answer and the two made love, going back to sleep once they finished. Akwasi-the-jealous-one returned, completely unaware of what had happened, and soon went to sleep as well.

However, his stomach troubled him again and again, and each time he called out to Anansi for help using the same name Anansi had given him. Akwasi-the-jealous-one would leave while Anansi snuck into their bedroom to make love with Aso. This happened a a total of nine times before morning came. Anansi left Akwasi's village when the next day arrived and did not return.

Two moons eventually passed and Aso was now clearly pregnant. Akwasi-the-jealous-one asked his wife how she'd gotten pregnant, because he was sterile and could not sire children with her. Aso told Akwasi that he in fact had told her to make love to Anansi, explaining that the child she'd conceived was his. Akwasi decided to take her to Nyame's village. However, Aso gave birth on the way, so she rested a moment. The two then took the child to Nyame's village after it was born and they told Nyame what had taken place.

Nyame did not believe the story and said that no one had left his village, urging them to point out the culprit among the villagers. Aso agreed to do so and soon saw Anansi sitting on a ridgepole in the distance. She pointed to Anansi and told Nyame that he was the one who'd impregnated her. Anansi moved further down on the ridgepole in an attempt to hide again, but Aso could still see him clearly. Under Aso's gaze Anansi fell over, dirtying himself thoroughly.

In return Anansi complained that their actions had defiled him, for he was Nyame's Soul-washer and Nyame's wishes had been ignored. As a result, Akwasi-the-jealous-one was seized by Nyame's subjects for disobeying the god's command and ordered Akwasi to sacrifice a sheep as penance. Utterly embarrassed, Akwasi made his sacrifice and then told the Sky-God that Anansi could have Aso, giving her to the Spider to become his wife.

There was still one more cost linked to what had transpired. The child Anansi had sired through Aso was taken and killed. What remained of its body was scattered throughout Nyame's village as a reminder that jealousy never pays. So it was that Aso became Anansi's wife, and jealousy came into the tribe.

THE FISH AND THE LEOPARD'S WIFE; OR, WHY THE FISH LIVES IN THE WATER

This story has been edited and adapted from Elphinstone Dayrell's Folk Stories From Southern Nigeria, first published in 1910 by Longmans, Green And Company, London And New York.

Many years ago, when King Eyo was ruler of Calabar, the fish used to live on the land. The fish was a great friend of the leopard, and frequently used to go to his house in the bush, where the leopard entertained him. Now the leopard had a very fine wife, with whom the fish fell in love. And after a time, whenever the leopard was absent in the bush, the fish used to go to his house and make love to the leopard's wife, until at last an old woman who lived near informed the leopard what happened whenever he went away.

At first the leopard would not believe that the fish, who had been his friend for so long, would play such a low trick, but one night he came back unexpectedly, and found the fish and his wife together. At this the leopard was very angry, and was going to kill the fish, but he thought as the fish had been his friend for so long, he would not deal with him himself, but would report his behaviour to King Eyo. This he did, and the king held a big palaver, at which the leopard stated his case quite shortly.

When the fish was put upon his defence he had nothing to say, so the king addressing his subjects said, "This is a very bad case, as the fish has been the leopard's friend, and has been trusted by him, but the fish has taken advantage of his friend's absence, and has betrayed him."

The king, therefore, made an order that for the future the fish should live in the water, and that if he ever came on the land he should die. He also said that all men and animals should kill and eat the fish whenever they could catch him, as a punishment for his behaviour with his friend's wife.

WHY MEN COMMIT EVIL AT NIGHT, CHILDREN PLAY IN MOONLIGHT, DISPUTES ARE SETTLED IN DAYTIME, AND ANANSI IS NYAME'S MESSENGER

This story has been edited and adapted from Captain R. S. Rattray's Akan-Ashanti Folk-Tales, first published in 1930 by Oxford University Press – American Branch, New York.

Nyame sired three children one day. Nyame raised Esum, or Night, Osrane, the Moon, and Owia, the Sun, well, and had them go out on their own. While each successfully built their own village, Nyame considered Owia his favourite child and wished to make him a chief. He harvested a yam known as "Kintinkyi" in secret, and decided that the son who could guess what it was would become chief and receive his royal stool as proof. Soon, Nyame blackened his royal stool and asked his subjects if any could guess what his thoughts were. Anansi happened to be there, and said that he knew. Nyame told Anansi to gather his sons from the villages, and Anansi left. However, Anansi didn't truly know, but secretly decided he would learn.

Anansi gathered feathers from every bird known and covered himself with them, and then flew above Nyame's village, startling the villagers. Nyame saw Anansi but did not recognize him within his disguise, and mused to himself that if Anansi were present, he'd know the name of the bird, because he'd said he knew that Nyame wished his son Owia to receive his stool and that he would give whomever could guess his yam's name the seat. He continued to ponder aloud while Anansi flew overheard and heard Nyame's plan and finally flew away, removing his disguise.

He went to Esum's village first and told him that his father wished to see him, but kept Nyame's plans secret. Night gave him roasted corn to eat as thanks and Anansi soon went to Osrane's village. Osrane was told the same, and he gave Anansi yam as thanks in return before the spider left for Owia's village, keeping the truth from Osrane as well. Soon, Anansi arrived and told Owia the same. Owia mentioned that he wished his father could see what he did so that he could know Owia's true intent, but decided he would treat Anansi the same, for his father had chosen him as his messenger and he wanted to treat him as he would his father, Nyame. Owia then prepared the best sheep for Anansi to eat as thanks, and in return Anansi decided to tell Owia of his father's intentions in secret, revealing the name of the yam he'd harvested.

Anansi then made a pair of drums that would shout the yam's name so that Owia would remember the name of Nyame's yam, which was Kintinkyi, and the two returned to the other sons of Nyame. Anansi brought them each before Nyame, and Nyame called an assembly together so they could welcome Anansi and Nyame's sons. Anansi said he'd completed Nyame's task, and the Sky-God revealed his intentions to his three sons. He then told Esum, who was oldest, that he would be allowed to guess first. Yet, Esum did not know, and said its name was "Pona". The villagers booed him. Osrane, the second-oldest, was given a chance, but he also failed to guess the yam's name, assuming it was called "Asante". The villagers booed him also. Owia, the youngest, was then given a chance to guess. Anansi played the drums as he had promised, and Owia remembered the true name of Nyame's yam, "Kintinkyi". The assembly cheered instead.

Nyame then spoke to Esum, his eldest son, and punished him, for he had not paid attention to him while Nyame had raised him. Evil things thus would be done during Esum's time. Next Nyame scolded Osrane, who had also not listened to him while he raised him. Only children would frolic during his time. Finally, Nyame spoke to his youngest son Owia, and praised him. Nyame made him chief and told him that any issue that needed to be settled would take place during his time. He gave him the rainbow to protect himself from his brothers if they ever wished to harm him, and promised that it would remind his subjects who saw it that danger would not befall them. Lastly, he gave Anansi his blessing for knowing his inner-thoughts, and said Anansi would be known as his messenger.

THE LITTLE CHILD AND THE PUMPKIN TREE

This story has been edited and adapted from the appendix of George Webbe Dasent's Popular Tales From The Norse, first published in 1907 by Edmonston and Douglas, based out of Edinburgh, Scotland.

There was once a poor widow who had six children. One day when she was going out to look for something to eat, for she was very poor, she met an old man sitting by the river side. He said to her "Good morning."

And she answered, "Good morning, father."

He said to her, "Will you wash my head?"

She said she would, so she washed it, and when she was going away, he gave her a 'stampee', a small coin, and told her to go a certain distance, and she would see a large tree full of pumpkins. She was then to dig a hole at the root of the tree and bury the money, and when she had done so, she was to call for as many pumpkins as she liked, and she should have them.

So the woman went, and did as she was told, and she called for six pumpkins, one for each child, and six came down, and she carried them home, and now they always had pumpkins enough to eat, for whenever they wanted any, the woman had only to go to the tree and call, and they had as many as they liked.

One morning when she got up, she found a little baby before the door, so she took it up and carried it in, and took care of it. Every day she went out, but in the morning she boiled enough pumpkins to serve the children all day. One day when she came back she found the food was all gone, so she scolded her children, and beat them for eating it all up. They told her they had not taken any, that it was the baby, but she would not believe them, and said, "How could a little baby get up and help itself".

But the children still persisted it was the baby. So one day when she was going out, she put some pumpkin in a calabash, and set a trap over it. When she was gone the baby got up as usual to eat the food, and got its head fastened in the trap, so that it could not get out, and began knocking its head about and crying out, "Oh! Do let me loose, for that woman will kill me when she comes back."

When the woman came in, she found the baby fastened in the trap, so she beat it well, and turned it out of doors, and begged her children's pardon for having wronged them.

Then after she turned the baby out, he changed into a great big man, and went to the river, where he saw the old man sitting by the river side, who asked him to wash his head, just as he had asked the poor woman, but the man said, "No, he would not wash his dirty head", and so he wished the old man "good bye".

Then the old man asked him if he would like to have a pumpkin, to which he said "yes", and the old man told him to go on till he saw a large tree with plenty of pumpkins on it, and then he must ask for one. So he went on till he got to the tree, and the pumpkins looked so nice he could not be satisfied with one, so he called out, "Ten pumpkins come down", and the ten pumpkins fell and crushed him.

DO NOT IMPOSE ON THE WEAK

This story has been edited and adapted from Robert Hamill Nassau's Where Animals Talk, first published in 1912 by Richard G. Badger at The Gorham Press, based out of Boston. This tale was originally told by storytellers from the Benga tribe.

Leopard and Chameleon lived apart. This one had his village, and that one his. This one did his own business, that one his. And they were resting quietly in their abodes. Chameleon had a herd of sheep and of goats.

Leopard came to the village of Chameleon on an excursion, and he saw the herd of sheep and of goats. He said to Chameleon, "Chum! give me a loan of sheep to raise on shares."

Chameleon made food for him, and, when they had eaten, he said to Leopard, "You can send children tomorrow, to come and take the loan of sheep on shares."

They had their conversation, talking, and talking. When they had ended, Leopard said, "My Fellow! I'm going back."

His friend said to him, "Very good."

Leopard went on to his village. He said, "My wife! I went on an excursion, to the town of Yongolokodi. He treated me with hospitality to the very greatest degree. Also he has given me sheep on shares."

The next day, in the morning, he sent his children to the town of Chameleon to take the herd of sheep. They went, and they brought them, and goats also.

The goats and sheep increased, until the village of Leopard was positively full of them and was crowded in abundance.

About three years passed, and Chameleon said to himself, "Our herd with Chum must be about sufficient for division."

Thereupon he started on his journey crawling, naka, naka, naka, until he came to the house of his friend Leopard. Leopard said to his wife, "Make food!" It was cooked, they ate, and rested.

Chameleon said to Leopard, "Chum! I have come, that we should divide the shares of the herd."

Leopard replied, "Good! But, first go back today. Who can catch goats and sheep on a hot day like this? Come tomorrow morning."

Chameleon said, "Very good." And he went back to his village.

The next day, in the morning, he rose to go to the village of Leopard. Actually, though, after midnight, Leopard had already opened the pens, and all the animals were scattered outside. He protested regret to Chameleon, and said, "Chum! Go back! I don't know how those fellows have opened their pens. I was expecting you, for this day; and I had let my herdsman know that a person was coming on the morrow. So, go back. And, as I am going tomorrow to the swamp for bamboo, you must come only on the second day."

Chameleon submissively replied, "Very good."

Chameleon continued coming, and his treatment was just so every time, with excuses. Leopard, hoping, said to himself, "Perhaps he will die on the way," because he saw him walking so slowly, naka, naka. And Chameleon kept on patiently going back and forth, back and forth.

One night, Leopard and his wife were lying down, when his wife asked him, "What is the reason that you and Yongolokodi have not divided the shares of the herd? Do you think he will die of this weakness?"

Leopard answered, "No! It is not weakness, Njambe is the one who created him so. It is his own way of walking."

Finally, Chameleon said to himself, "I must see what Njâ intends to do to me, whether he thinks that he shall eat my share."

He went by night and waited outside of Leopard's. Next day, in the morning, as Leopard rose to go out, he found, unexpectedly, as he emerged from the house, Chameleon sitting on the threshold. There was no other deception that Leopard could seek, for, the animals were still in their pens. So, he called his children, and said, "Tie the goats and sheep with cords."

So they tied them all. And he and Chameleon divided them. Then this one returned to his place, and that one to his.

THE ORPHAN BOY AND THE MAGIC STONE

This story has been edited and adapted from Elphinstone Dayrell's Folk Stories From Southern Nigeria, first published in 1910 by Longmans, Green And Company, London And New York.

A chief of Inde named Inkita had a son named Ayong Kita, whose mother had died at his birth.

The old chief was a hunter, and used to take his son out with him when he went into the bush. He used to do most of his hunting in the long grass which grows over nearly all the Inde country, and used to kill plenty of bush buck in the dry season.

In those days the people had no guns, so the chief had to shoot everything he got with his bow and arrows, which required a lot of skill.

When his little son was old enough, he gave him a small bow and some small arrows, and taught him how to shoot. The little boy was very quick at learning, and by continually practising at lizards and small birds, soon became expert in the use of his little bow, and could hit them almost every time he shot at them.

When the boy was ten years old his father died, and as he thus became the head of his father's house, and was in authority over all the slaves, they became very discontented, and made plans to kill him, so he ran away into the bush.

Having nothing to eat, he lived for several days on the nuts which fell from the palm trees. He was too young to kill any large animals, and only had his small bow and arrows, with which he killed a few squirrels, bush rats, and small birds, and so managed to live.

Now once at night, when he was sleeping in the hollow of a tree, he had a dream in which his father appeared, and told him where there was plenty of treasure buried in the earth, but, being a small boy, he was frightened, and did not go to the place.

One day, sometime after the dream, having walked far and being very thirsty, he went to a lake, and was just going to drink, when he heard a hissing sound, and heard a voice tell him not to drink. Not seeing any one, he was afraid, and ran away without drinking.

Early next morning, when he was out with his bow trying to shoot some small animal, he met an old woman with quite long hair. She was so ugly that he thought she must be a witch, so he tried to run, but she told him not to fear, as she wanted to help him and assist him to rule over his late father's house. She also told him that it was she who had called out to him at the lake not to drink, as there was a bad Ju-Ju in the water which would have killed him.

The old woman then took Ayong to a stream some little distance from the lake, and bending down, took out a small shining stone from the water, which she gave to him, at the same time telling him to go to the place which his father had advised him to visit in his dream. She then said, "When you get there you must dig, and you will find plenty of money. You must then go and buy two strong slaves, and when you have got them, you must take them into the forest, away from the town, and get them to build you a house with several rooms in it. You must then place the stone in one of the rooms, and whenever you want anything, all you have to do is to go into the room and tell the stone what you want, and your wishes will be at once gratified."

Ayong did as the old woman told him, and after much difficulty and danger bought the two slaves and built a house in the forest, taking great care of the precious stone, which he placed in an inside room. Then for some time, whenever he wanted anything, he used to go into the room and ask for a sufficient number of rods to buy what he wanted, and they were always brought at once.

This went on for many years, and Ayong grew up to be a man, and became very rich, and bought many slaves, having made friends with the Aro men, who in those days used to do a big traffic in slaves. After ten years had passed Ayong had quite a large town and many slaves, but one night the old woman appeared to him in a dream and told him that she thought that he was sufficiently wealthy, and that it was time for him to return the magic stone to the small stream from whence it came.

But Ayong, although he was rich, wanted to rule his father's house and be a head chief for all the Inde country, so he sent for all the Ju-Ju men in the country and two witch men, and marched with all his slaves to his father's town. Before he started he held a big palaver, and told them to point out any slave who had a bad heart, and who might kill him when he came to rule the country. Then the Ju-Ju men consulted together, and pointed out fifty of the slaves who, they said, were witches, and would try to kill Ayong. He at once had them made prisoners, and tried them by the ordeal of Esere bean, which is trial by poison, to see whether they were witches or not. As none of them could vomit the beans they all died, and were declared to be witches. He then had them buried at once.

When the remainder of his slaves saw what had happened, they all came to him and begged his pardon, and promised to serve him faithfully. Although the fifty men were buried they could not rest, and troubled Ayong very much, and after a time he became very sick himself, so he sent again for the Ju-Ju men, who told him that it was the witch men who, although they were dead and buried, had power to come out at night and used to suck Ayong's blood, which was the cause of his sickness. They then said, "We are only three Ju-Ju men. you must get seven more of us, making the magic number of ten."

When they came they dug up the bodies of the fifty witches, and found they were quite fresh. Then Ayong had big fires made, and burned them one after the other, and gave the Ju-Ju men a big present. He soon after became quite well again, and took possession of his father's property, and ruled over all the country.

Ever since then, whenever anyone is accused of being a witch, they are tried by the ordeal of the poisonous Esere bean, and if they can vomit they do not die, and are declared innocent, but if they cannot do so, they die in great pain.

BORROWED CLOTHES

This story has been edited and adapted from Robert Hamill Nassau's Where Animals Talk, first published in 1912 by Richard G. Badger at The Gorham Press, based out of Boston. This tale was originally told by storytellers from the Benga tribe.

Parrot and Chicken were fowls living in a village of Mankind near a town, which they had built together. They were living there in great friendship.

Then Parrot said to Chicken, "Chum! I'm going to make an engagement for marriage."

So, he prepared his journey. And he asked Chicken, "Chum! Give me now your fine dress!"

Chicken, said, "Very good!" and he handed his tail feathers to him.

Thereupon, Parrot went on his marriage journey.

When he came home again, he said to himself, "These feathers become me. I will not return them to Kuba."

So, when Chicken said to him, "Return me my clothes," he replied, "I will not return them!"

Chicken, seeing that Parrot was retaining the feathers, said sarcastically, "Accept your clothing!"

Thereupon, Parrot, pretending to be wronged, said, "Fellow! Why do you put me to shame? I did not say that I would take your clothing altogether, only that we should exchange clothes."

At night, then, Parrot took all his family, and they flew up in the air and far away. At once, he decided to stay there, and did not come to live on the ground again. Chicken was left with Mankind in the town.

Whenever Chicken began to call to Parrot up in the treetops, asking for his clothes, Parrot only screamed back "Wâ! Wâ!" That was a mode of speech by which to mock at Chicken.

THE LION, THE GOAT, AND THE BABOON

This story has been edited and adapted from the appendix of George Webbe Dasent's Popular Tales From The Norse, first published in 1907 by Edmonston and Douglas, based out of Edinburgh, Scotland.

A Lion had a Goat for his wife. One day Goat went out to market, and while she was gone, Lion went out in the wood, where he met with Baboon, who made friends with Lion, for fear he would eat him, and asked him to go home with him, but the Lion thought it would be a good chance, so he asked the Baboon to go home with him and see his little ones.

When they got home, the Baboon said to the Lion, "Why, you have got plenty of little goats here."

The Lion said, "Yes, they are my children."

So the Baboon said, "If they are, they are little goats, and they are very good meat."

So the Lion said, "Don't make a noise. Their mother will come presently, and we will see."

So these little goats took no notice, but went out to meet their mother, and told her what had passed.

Their mother said to them, "Go back, take no notice, and I shall come home presently, and shall do for him."

So she went and bought some molasses, and took it home with her.

The Lion said, "Are you come? What news?"

"Oh!" she said, "good news, taste here."

He tasted, and said, "It's very good, it's honey."

And she said, "It's baboon's blood. They have been killing one today, the blood is running in the street, and everyone is carrying it away."

The Lion said, "Hush, there's one in the house, and we shall have him."

At this the Baboon rushed off, and when they looked for him, he was gone, and never came near them again, which saved the little goats' lives.

THE STORY OF THE LIGHTNING AND THE THUNDER

This story has been edited and adapted from Elphinstone Dayrell's Folk Stories From Southern Nigeria, first published in 1910 by Longmans, Green And Company, London And New York.

In the olden days the thunder and lightning lived on the earth amongst all the other people, but the king made them live at the far end of the town, as far as possible from other people's houses.

The thunder was an old mother sheep, and the lightning was her son, a ram. Whenever the ram got angry he used to go about and burn houses and knock down trees. He even did damage on the farms, and sometimes killed people. Whenever the lightning did these things, his mother used to call out to him in a very loud voice to stop and not to do any more damage, but the lightning did not care in the least for what his mother said, and when he was in a bad temper used to do a very large amount of damage. At last the people could not stand it any longer, and complained to the king.

So the king made a special order that sheep Thunder and her son, ram Lightning, should leave the town and live in the far bush. This did not do much good, as when the ram got angry he still burnt the forest, and the flames sometimes spread to the farms and consumed them.

So the people complained again, and the king banished both the lightning and the thunder from the earth and made them live in the sky, where they could not cause so much destruction. Ever since, when the lightning is angry, he commits damage as before, but you can hear his mother, the thunder, rebuking him and telling him to stop. Sometimes, however, when the mother has gone away some distance from her naughty son, you can still see that he is angry and is doing damage, but his mother's voice cannot be heard.

A LESSON IN EVOLUTION

This story has been edited and adapted from Robert Hamill Nassau's Where Animals Talk, first published in 1912 by Richard G. Badger at The Gorham Press, based out of Boston. This tale was originally told by storytellers from the Fang tribe.

Shrew and Lemur were neighbours in the town of Beasts. At that time, the Animals did not possess fire.

Lemur said to Shrew, "Go and take for us fire from the town of Mankind."

Shrew consented, but said, "If I go, do not look, while I am gone, toward any other place except the path on which I go. Do not even wink. Watch for me."

So Shrew went, and came to a Town of Men, and found that the people had all emigrated from that town. Yet, he went on, and on, seeking for fire, and for a long time found none. But, as he continued moving forward from house to house, he at last found a very little fire on a hearth. He began blowing it, and kept on blowing, and blowing, for the fire did not soon ignite into a flame. He continued so long at this that his mouth extended forward permanently, with the blowing.

Then he went back, and found Lemur faithfully watching with his eyes standing very wide open.

Shrew asked him, "What has made your eyes so big?"

In return, Lemur asked him, "What has so lengthened your mouth to a snout?"

WHY DEAD PEOPLE ARE BURIED

This story has been edited and adapted from Elphinstone Dayrell's Folk Stories From Southern Nigeria, first published in 1910 by Longmans, Green And Company, London And New York.

In the beginning of the world when the Creator had made men and women and the animals, they all lived together in the creation land. The Creator was a big chief, past all men, and being very kind-hearted, was very sorry whenever anyone died. So one day he sent for the dog, who was his head messenger, and told him to go out into the world and give his word to all people that for the future whenever anyone died the body was to be placed in the compound, and wood ashes were to be thrown over it, and that the dead body was to be left on the ground, and in twenty-four hours it would become alive again.

When the dog had travelled for half a day he began to get tired, so as he was near an old woman's house he looked in, and seeing a bone with some meat on it he made a meal of it, and then went to sleep, entirely forgetting the message which had been given him to deliver.

After a time, when the dog did not return, the Creator called for a sheep, and sent him out with the same message. But the sheep was a very foolish one, and being hungry, began eating the sweet grasses by the wayside. After a time, however, he remembered that he had a message to deliver, but forgot what it was exactly, so as he went about among the people he told them that the message the Creator had given him to tell the people, was that whenever anyone died they should be buried underneath the ground.

A little time afterwards the dog remembered his message, so he ran into the town and told the people that they were to place wood ashes on the dead bodies and leave them in the compound, and that they would come to life again after twenty-four hours. But the people would not believe him, and said, "We have already received the word from the Creator by the sheep, that all dead bodies should be buried."

In consequence of this the dead bodies are now always buried, and the dog is much disliked and not trusted as a messenger, because if he had not found the bone in the old woman's house and forgotten his message, the dead people might still be alive.

HOW ANANSI GOT A BALD HEAD

This story has been edited and adapted from Captain R. S. Rattray's Akan-Ashanti Folk-Tales, first published in 1930 by Oxford University Press – American Branch, New York.

Sometime after they were married, it is said Kwaku Anansi the Spider and his wife Aso were living together. One day, they had returned from a visit to the plantation outside of the village, when a messenger came to them. Anansi approached the messenger and asked him why he'd come, and the man responded that Anansi's mother-in-law had died the previous day. In response Anansi told his wife Aso what had taken place, and told Aso that they would go to the village to mourn her mother, as the funeral would take place within a few days.

Soon the messenger left, and the next morning came. Anansi spared no time and went to the others in the village for a favour and found Odwan the Sheep, Okra the Cat, Okraman the Dog, Akoko the Fowl, and Aberekyie the Goat. Anansi told them of his mother-in-law's passing and asked if they could accompany him to her funeral, and they agreed. Anansi thanked them, and then returned to his home to prepare.

Anansi made clothes to wear to the funeral, sewing a hat from leopard's skin. He dyed his cloth russet, and had the attire he wished to wear prepared. Thursday eventually came and it was time to head out toward the village where the funeral of Aso's mother would take place. He called those who'd agreed to accompany him, and they left the village, but not without supplies of guns, drums, palm-wine, and other things so that they would have things to share with the rest of those who attended as they celebrated his mother-in-law's memory.

Soon, Anansi and his people reached his mother-in-law's village and fired their guns in the air to signal they had arrived, and they went to the home where her wake was taking place. Anansi shared all that he'd brought, giving palm-wine to those mourning. He then presented an offering to help pay for the funeral, which was six peredwan packets of gold dust, a velvet pillow, two cloths, a wool blanket, shell money for bartering with ghosts, a sheep, and more palm-wine. They accepted his offer, and the others matched it.

The next morning, everyone ate and invited Anansi to eat as well. However, Anansi said that he was not allowed to, as it was his mother-in-law's funeral and he would not eat until the eighth day. Instead, Anansi said he'd gather some for his neighbours who'd accompanied him and remain while they left. True to his word, Anansi asked Aso to find them food and she brought it to them. Anansi bade them farewell, and he remained at the home.

Days passed and he resisted eating, but when the fourth day came, he was too hungry to resist eating, and went to search for food inside the home where he was staying. He went into the kitchen and saw that there was a fire going, and at that fire there were beans boiling in a pot. Anansi decided he would eat those, so he took his leopard hat and scooped some of the beans inside once he was sure no one was watching him. However, just as soon as he put on his hat to hide the beans, he saw Aso enter the room. Startled, Anansi hatched up another plan and told Aso that a hat-shaking festival was taking place in his father's village, and he intended to go there himself. Aso became suspicious and asked Anansi why he had not told her of the festival before. She reminded him that he had not eaten anything and advised the Spider to wait until the next day. However, Anansi refused to listen to his wife's advice and she stormed off.

Aso gathered the people in the village and told them what Anansi was planning so they could hopefully keep him from leaving, and then headed back to her husband. Anansi saw Aso returning with the crowd and grabbed his hat, singing:

"Just now at my father's village they are shaking hats!

Saworowa, they are shaking hats!

E, they are shaking hats,

O, they are shaking hats!

Saworowa!"

Anansi began to panic, because the beans in his leopard's hat were burning him, and he told them he was leaving and would not remain whatsoever. Anansi left, but the villagers followed him, even when he told them to leave. In panic he sang again:

"Turn back, because

"Just now at my father's village they are shaking hats!

Saworowa, they are shaking hats!

E, they are shaking hats,

O, they are shaking hats!

Saworowa!"

Now, the beans were unbearably hot upon his head, so Anansi threw his hat with its beans away. When Aso realized what Anansi had done, she and the villagers booed him and he ran away down the road. He promised the road that he would thank it if it helped him escape, and it agreed to, leading him away from the villagers and to medicine he could use. So it is that Anansi has a bald head, from the airs he gave himself during his mother-in-law's funeral.

THE DANCING GANG

This story has been edited and adapted from the appendix of George Webbe Dasent's Popular Tales From The Norse, first published in 1907 by Edmonston and Douglas, based out of Edinburgh, Scotland.

A water carrier once went to the river to fetch water. She dipped in her calabash, and brought out a cray-fish. The cray-fish began beating his claws on the calabash, and played such a beautiful tune, that the girl began dancing, and could not stop.

The driver of the gang wondered why she did not come, and sent another to see where she might be. When she came, she too began to dance. So the driver sent another, who also began to dance when she heard the music and the cray-fish singing:

"Stay for us, stay for us,

how long will you stay for us?"

Then the driver sent another and another, till he had sent the whole gang.

At last he went himself, and when he found the whole gang dancing, he too began to dance, and they all danced till night, when the cray-fish went back into the water, and if they haven't done dancing, they are dancing still.

A CHAIN OF CIRCUMSTANCES

This story has been edited and adapted from Robert Hamill Nassau's Where Animals Talk, first published in 1912 by Richard G. Badger at The Gorham Press, based out of Boston. This tale was originally told by storytellers from the Fang tribe.

Tortoise was a blacksmith, and allowed other people to use his bellows. Cockroach had a spear that was known of by all people and things. One day, he went to the smithy at the village of Tortoise. When he started to work the bellows, as he looked out in the street, he saw Chicken coming, and he said to Tortoise, "I'm afraid of Kuba, that he will catch me. What shall I do?"

So Tortoise told him, "Go and hide yourself off there in the grass."

At once he hid himself. Then Chicken arrived, and he, observing a spear lying on the ground, asked Tortoise, "Is not this Etanda's Spear?"

Tortoise assented, "Yes, do you want him?"

And Chicken said, "Yes, where is he?"

So Tortoise said, "He hid himself in the grass on the ground yonder. Catch him."

Then Chicken went and caught Cockroach, and swallowed him.

When Chicken was about to go away to return to his place, Tortoise said to him, "Come back! Work for me at this fine bellows!"

As Chicken, willing to return a favour, was about to stand at it, he looked around and saw Genet coming in the street. Chicken said to Tortoise, "Alas! I'm afraid that Uhingi will see me, where shall I go?"

So, Tortoise said, "Go and hide!"

Chicken did so. When Genet came, he, seeing the spear, asked, "Is it not so that this is Etanda's Spear?"

Tortoise replied, "Yes."

Genet asked him, "Where is Etanda?"

He replied, "Chicken has swallowed him."

Genet inquired, "And where is Chicken?"

Tortoise showed him the place where Chicken was hidden. And Genet went and caught and ate Chicken.

When Genet was about to go, Tortoise called to him, "No! Come to work this fine bellows."

Genet set to work, but, when he looked into the street, he hesitated; for, he saw Leopard coming. Genet said to Tortoise, "I must go, lest Nje should see me!"

Then Tortoise said, "Go and hide in the grass."

So, Genet hid himself in the grass.

Leopard, having arrived and wondering about the Spear, asked Tortoise, "Is it not so that this is the Spear of Etanda?"

Tortoise answered, "Yes."

Then Leopard asked, "Where is Etanda?"

Tortoise replied, "Kuba has swallowed him."

"And, where is Kuba?"

Tortoise answered, "Uhingi has eaten him."

Then Leopard asked, "Where then is Uhingi?"

Tortoise asked, "Do you want him? Go and catch him! He is hidden yonder there."

Then Leopard caught and killed Genet.

Leopard was going away, but Tortoise told him, "Wait! Come to work this fine bellows."

When Leopard was about to comply, he looked around the street, and he saw a Human Being coming with a gun carried on his shoulder. Leopard exclaimed, "Kudu-O! I do not want to see a Man, let me go!"

Then Tortoise said to him, "Go and hide."

Leopard did so.

When the Man had come, and he saw the Spear of Cockroach, he inquired, "Is it not so that this is Cockroach's wonderful Spear?"

Tortoise answered, "Yes."

And the Man asked, "Where then is Cockroach?"

Tortoise answered, "Kuba has swallowed him."

Man asked, "And where is Chicken?"

Tortoise answered, "Uhingi has eaten him."

Man asked, "And where is Genet?"

Tortoise answered, "Nje has killed him."

Man asked, "And where is Leopard?"

Tortoise did not at once reply, and Man asked again, "Where is Leopard?"

The Tortoise said, "Do you want him? Go and catch him. He has hidden himself over there."

Then the Man went and shot Leopard, who had killed Genet, who had eaten Chicken, who had swallowed Cockroach, who owned the wonderful Spear, and all at the smithy of Tortoise.

WHY THE BAT IS ASHAMED TO BE SEEN IN THE DAYTIME

This story has been edited and adapted from Elphinstone Dayrell's Folk Stories From Southern Nigeria, first published in 1910 by Longmans, Green And Company, London And New York.

There was once an old mother sheep who had seven lambs, and one day the bat, who was about to make a visit to his father-in-law who lived a long day's march away, went to the old sheep and asked her to lend him one of her young lambs to carry his load for him. At first the mother sheep refused, but as the young lamb was anxious to travel and see something of the world, and begged to be allowed to go, at last she reluctantly consented.

So in the morning at daylight the bat and the lamb set off together, the lamb carrying the bat's drinking-horn. When they reached half-way, the bat told the lamb to leave the horn underneath a bamboo tree. Directly he arrived at the house, he sent the lamb back to get the horn. When the lamb had gone the bat's father-in-law brought him food, and the bat ate it all, leaving nothing for the lamb.

When the lamb returned, the bat said to him, "Hello! You have arrived at last I see, but you are too late for food, for it is all finished."

He then sent the lamb back to the tree with the horn, and when the lamb returned again it was late, and he went to bed quite supperless. The next day, just before it was time for food, the bat sent the lamb off again for the drinking-horn, and when the food arrived the bat, who was very greedy, ate it all up a second time. This mean behaviour on the part of the bat went on for four days, until at last the lamb became quite thin and weak. The bat decided to return home the next day, and it was all the lamb could do to carry his load.

When he got home to his mother the lamb complained bitterly of the treatment he had received from the bat, and was baa-ing all night, complaining of pains in his inside. The old mother sheep, who was very fond of her children, determined to be revenged on the bat for the cruel way he had starved her lamb. She decided to consult the tortoise, who, although very poor, was considered by all people to be the wisest of all animals. When the old sheep had told the whole story to the tortoise, he considered for some time, and then told the sheep that she might leave the matter entirely to him, and he would take ample revenge on the bat for his cruel treatment of her son.

Very soon after this the bat thought he would again go and see his father-in-law, so he went to the mother sheep again and asked her for one of her sons to carry his load as before. The tortoise, who happened to be present, told the bat that he was going in that direction, and would cheerfully carry his load for him. They set out on their journey the following day, and when they arrived at the half-way halting-place the bat pursued the same tactics that he had on the previous occasion. He told the tortoise to hide his drinking-horn under the same tree as the lamb had hidden it before, and this the tortoise did, but when the bat was not looking he picked up the drinking-horn again and hid it in his bag.

When they arrived at the house the tortoise hung the horn up out of sight in the back yard, and then sat down in the house. Just before it was time for food the bat sent the tortoise to get the drinking-horn, and the tortoise went outside into the yard, and waited until he heard that the beating of the boiled yams into foo-foo had finished. He then went into the house and gave the drinking-horn to the bat, who was so surprised and angry, that when the food was passed he refused to eat any of it, so the tortoise ate it all. This went on for four days, until at last the bat became as thin as the poor little lamb had been on the previous occasion.

At last the bat could stand the pains of his inside no longer, and secretly told his mother-in-law to bring him food when the tortoise was not looking. He said, "I am now going to sleep for a little, but you can wake me up when the food is ready."

The tortoise, who had been listening all the time, being hidden in a corner out of sight, waited until the bat was fast asleep, and then carried him very gently into the next room and placed him on his own bed. He then very softly and quietly took off the bat's cloth and covered himself in it, and lay down where the bat had been. Very soon the bat's mother-in-law brought the food and placed it next to where the bat was supposed to be sleeping, and having pulled his cloth to wake him, went away. The tortoise then got up and ate all the food. When he had finished he carried the bat back again, and took some of the palm-oil and foo-foo and placed it inside the bat's lips while he was asleep. Then the tortoise went to sleep himself.

In the morning when he woke up the bat was more hungry than ever, and in a very bad temper, so he sought out his mother-in-law and started scolding her, and asked her why she had not brought his food as he had told her to do. She replied that she had brought his food, and that he had eaten it, but this the bat denied, and accused the tortoise of having eaten the food. The woman then said she would call the people in and they should decide the matter, but the tortoise slipped out first and told the people that the best way to find out who had eaten the food was to make both the bat and himself rinse their mouths out with clean water into a basin. This they decided to do, so the tortoise got his tooth-stick which he always used, and having cleaned his teeth properly, washed his mouth out, and returned to the house.

When all the people had arrived the woman told them how the bat had abused her, and as he still maintained that he had had no food for five days, the people said that both he and the tortoise should wash their mouths out with clean water into two clean calabashes. This was done, and at once it could clearly be seen that the bat had been eating, as there were distinct traces of the palm-oil and foo-foo, which the tortoise had put inside his lips, floating on the water. When the people saw this they decided against the bat, and he was so ashamed that he ran away then and there, and has ever since always hidden himself in the bush during the daytime, so that no one could see him, and only comes out at night to get his food.

The next day the tortoise returned to the mother sheep and told her what he had done, and that the bat was for ever disgraced. The old sheep praised him very much, and told all her friends, in consequence of which the reputation of the tortoise for wisdom was greatly increased throughout the whole country.

THE BROTHER AND HIS SISTERS

This story has been edited and adapted from the appendix of George Webbe Dasent's Popular Tales From The Norse, first published in 1907 by Edmonston and Douglas, based out of Edinburgh, Scotland.

There were once upon a time three sisters and a brother. The sisters were all proud, and one was very beautiful, and she did not like her little brother, "because", she said, "he was dirty". Now, this beautiful sister was to be married, and the brother begged their mother not to let her marry, as he was sure the man would kill her, for he knew his house was full of bones. So the mother told her daughter, but she would not believe it, and said, "she wouldn't listen to anything that such a dirty little scrub said", and so she was married.

Now, it was agreed that one sister was to remain with their mother and the other was to go with the bride, and so they set out on their way. When they got to the beach, the husband picked up a beautiful tortoise-shell comb, which he gave to his bride. Then they got into his boat and rowed away over the sea, and when they reached their home, they were so surprised to see the little brother, for the comb had turned into the brother. They were not at all glad to see him, and the husband thought to himself he would kill him without telling his wife. When night came the boy told the husband that at home his mother always put him to sleep in the blacksmith's shop, and so the husband said he should sleep in the smithy.

In the middle of the night the man got up, intending to kill them all, and went to his shop to get his irons ready, but the boy jumped up as soon as he went in, and the man said, "Boy, what is the matter with you?"

So the boy said, when he was at home his mother always gave him two bags of gold to put his head on. Then the man said, he should have them, and went and fetched him two bags of gold, and told him to go to sleep.

But the boy said, "Now mind, when you hear me snore I'm not asleep, but when I am not snoring, then I'm asleep."

Then the boy went to sleep and began to snore, and as long as the man heard the snoring, he blew his bellows, but as soon as the snoring stopped, the man took his irons out of the fire, and the boy jumped up.

Then the man said, "Why, what's the matter? Why, can't you sleep?"

The boy said "No, for at home my mother always gave me four bags of money to lie upon."

Well, the man said he should have them, and brought him four bags of money. Then the boy told him again the same thing about his snoring and the man bade him go to sleep, and he began to snore, and the man to blow his bellows until the snoring stopped. Then the man took out his irons again, and the boy jumped up, and the man dropped the irons, saying, "Why, what's the matter now that you can't sleep?"

The boy said, "At home my mother always gave me two bushels of corn."

So the man said he should have the corn, and went and brought it, and told him to go to sleep. Then the boy snored, and the man blew his bellows till the snoring stopped, when he again took out his irons, and the boy jumped up, and the man said, "Why, what is it now?"

The boy said, "At home my mother always goes to the river with a sieve to bring me some water."

So the man said "Very well, I will go, but I have a cock here, and before I go, I must speak to it."

Then the man told the cock if he saw any one moving in the house, he must crow. The cock promised to do just that, and the man set off.

Now when the boy thought the man was gone far away, he got up, and gave the cock some of the corn. Then he woke up his sisters and showed them all the bones the man had in the house, and they were very frightened. Then he took the two bags of gold on his shoulders, and told his sisters to follow him. He took them to the bay, and put them into the boat with the bags of gold, and left them whilst he went back for the four bags of money. When he was leaving the house he emptied the bags of corn for the cock, who was so busy eating, he forget to crow, until they had got quite away.

When the man returned home and could not find any of them in the house, so he went to the river, where he found his boat gone, and so he had no way of going after them. When they landed at their own place, the boy turned the boat over and stove it in, so that it was of no use any more, and he took his sisters home, and told their mother all that had happened, and his sisters loved him, and they lived very happily together ever afterwards, and do so still if they are not dead.

WHY THE MOON WAXES AND WANES

This story has been edited and adapted from Elphinstone Dayrell's Folk Stories From Southern Nigeria, first published in 1910 by Longmans, Green And Company, London And New York.

There was once an old woman who was very poor, and lived in a small mud hut thatched with mats made from the leaves of the tombo palm in the bush. She was often very hungry, as there was no one to look after her.

In the olden days the moon used often to come down to the earth, although she lived most of the time in the sky. The moon was a fat woman with a skin of hide, and she was full of fat meat. She was quite round, and in the night used to give plenty of light. The moon was sorry for the poor starving old woman, so she came to her and said, "You may cut some of my meat away for your food."

This the old woman did every evening, and the moon got smaller and smaller until you could scarcely see her at all. Of course this made her give very little light, and all the people began to grumble in consequence, and to ask why it was that the moon was getting so thin.

At last the people went to the old woman's house where there happened to be a little girl sleeping. She had been there for some little time, and had seen the moon come down every evening, and the old woman go out with her knife and carve her daily supply of meat out of the moon. As she was very frightened, she told the people all about it, so they determined to set a watch on the movements of the old woman.

That very night the moon came down as usual, and the old woman went out with her knife and basket to get her food, but before she could carve any meat all the people rushed out shouting, and the moon was so frightened that she went back again into the sky, and never came down again to the earth. The old woman was left to starve in the bush.

Ever since that time the moon has hidden herself most of the day, as she was so frightened, and she still gets very thin once a month, but later on she gets fat again, and when she is quite fat she gives plenty of light all the night, but this does not last very long, and she begins to get thinner and thinner, in the same way as she did when the old woman was carving her meat from her.

ITUEN AND THE KING'S WIFE

This story has been edited and adapted from Elphinstone Dayrell's Folk Stories From Southern Nigeria, first published in 1910 by Longmans, Green And Company, London And New York.

Ituen was a young man of Calabar. He was the only child of his parents, and they were extremely fond of him, as he was of fine proportions and very good to look upon. They were poor people, and when Ituen grew up and became a man, he had very little money indeed, in fact he had so little food, that every day it was his custom to go to the market carrying an empty bag, into which he used to put anything eatable he could find after the market was over.

At this time Offiong was king. He was an old man, but he had plenty of wives. One of these women, named Attem, was quite young and very good-looking. She did not like her old husband, but wished for a young and handsome husband. She therefore told her servant to go round the town and the market to try and find such a man and to bring him at night by the side door to her house, and she herself would let him in, and would take care that her husband did not discover him.

That day the servant went all round the town, but failed to find any young man good-looking enough. She was just returning to report her ill-success when, on passing through the market-place, she saw Ituen picking up the remains of corn and other things which had been left on the ground. She was immediately struck with his fine appearance and strength, and saw that he was just the man to make a proper lover for her mistress, so she went up to him, and said that the queen had sent for him, as she was so taken with his good looks. At first Ituen was frightened and refused to go, as he knew that if the King discovered him he would be killed. However, after much persuasion he consented, and agreed to go to the queen's side door when it was dark.

When night came he went with great fear and trembling, and knocked very softly at the queen's door. The door was opened at once by the queen herself, who was dressed in all her best clothes, and had many necklaces, beads, and anklets on. Directly she saw Ituen she fell in love with him at once, and praised his good looks and his shapely limbs. She then told her servant to bring water and clothes, and after he had had a good wash and put on a clean cloth, he re-joined the queen. She hid him in her house all the night.

In the morning when he wished to go she would not let him, but, although it was very dangerous, she hid him in the house, and secretly conveyed food and clothes to him. Ituen stayed there for two weeks, and then he said that it was time for him to go and see his mother, but the queen persuaded him to stay another week, much against his will.

When the time came for him to depart, the queen got together fifty carriers with presents for Ituen's mother who, she knew, was a poor woman. Ten slaves carried three hundred rods; the other forty carried yams, pepper, salt, tobacco, and cloth. When all the presents arrived Ituen's mother was very pleased and embraced her son, and noticed with pleasure that he was looking well, and was dressed in much finer clothes than usual, but when she heard that he had attracted the queen's attention she was frightened, as she knew the penalty imposed on any one who attracted the attention of one of the king's wives.

Ituen stayed for a month in his parents' house and worked on the farm, but the queen could not be without her lover any longer, so she sent for him to go to her at once. Ituen went again, and, as before, arrived at night, when the queen was delighted to see him again.

In the middle of the night some of the king's servants, who had been told the story by the slaves who had carried the presents to Ituen's mother, came into the queen's room and surprised her there with Ituen. They hastened to the king, and told him what they had seen. Ituen was then made a prisoner, and the king sent out to all his people to attend at the palaver house to hear the case tried. He also ordered eight Egbos to attend armed with machetes. When the case was tried Ituen was found guilty, and the king told the eight Egbo men to take him into the bush and deal with him according to native custom. The Egbos then took Ituen into the bush and tied him up to a tree. Then with a sharp knife they cut off his lower jaw, and carried it to the king.

When the queen heard the fate of her lover she was very sad, and cried for three days. This made the king angry, so he told the Egbos to deal with his wife and her servant according to their law. They took the queen and the servant into the bush, where Ituen was still tied up to the tree dying and in great pain. Then, as the queen had nothing to say in her defence, they tied her and the girl up to different trees, and cut the queen's lower jaw off in the same way as they had her lover's. The Egbos then put out both the eyes of the servant, and left all three to die of starvation.

The king then made an Egbo law that for the future no one belonging to Ituen's family was to go into the market on market day, and that no one was to pick up the rubbish in the market. The king made an exception to the law in favour of the vulture and the dog, who were not considered very fine people, and would not be likely to run off with one of the king's wives, and that is why you still find vultures and dogs scavenging in the market-places even at the present time.

HISTORICAL NOTES

This section contains some brief biographical notes about the original collectors and their books featured in this collection. These notes have been adapted from those primarily on Wikipedia along with other supporting sources and notes.

Elphinstone Dayrell

Elphinstone Dayrell was born in 1869 and later became District Commissioner at Ikom, Eastern Province, in Nigeria. He was also a Fellow of the Royal Geographical Society and Fellow of the Royal Anthropological Institute. He died in 1917.

Folk Stories from Southern Nigeria was published in 1910. The book contains forty folk stories and fairy tales from Southern Nigeria. The book has an introduction by Andrew Lang, famous for his series of fairy books.

George Webbe Dasent

Dasent was born in May 1817 at St. Vincent, British West Indies, the son of the attorney general, John Roche Dasent. His mother was the second wife of his father. Charlotte Martha was the daughter of Captain Alexander Burrowes Irwin.

Dasent was educated at Westminster School, King's College London, and Oxford University, where he befriended classmate J.T. Delane, later to become his brother-in-law. After graduating from university in 1840 with a degree in Classical literature, he was appointed secretary to Thomas Cartwright on a diplomatic post in Stockholm, Sweden. There he met Jakob Grimm, at whose recommendation he first became interested in Scandinavian literature and mythology.

He published the first result of his studies, an English translation of *The Prose or Younger Edda* in 1842, followed by a translation of Rask's *Grammar of the Icelandic or Old-Norse Tongue* in 1843.

Returning to England in 1845 he became assistant editor of *The Times* under his schoolmate Delane, whose sister he married. Dasent's connections to Prussian diplomat Bunsen has been credited with significantly contributing to the paper developing its editorial policy towards foreign policy. While working for the newspaper, Dasent still continued his Scandinavian studies, publishing translations of various Norse stories. He also read for the Bar and was called in 1852.

In 1853, he was appointed professor of English literature and modern history at King's College London and in 1859 he translated *Popular Tales from the Norse (Norske Folkeeventyr)* by Peter Christen Asbjørnsen and Jørgen Moe, including in it an *Introductory Essay on the Origin and Diffusion of Popular Tales.*"

Perhaps his most well-known work, *The Story of Burnt Njal*, a translation of the Icelandic *Njal's Saga* that he had first attempted while in Stockholm, was issued in 1861. This work established sustained interest in Icelandic literature, so that more translations would follow. Dasent made a visit during 1861-1862 to Iceland, where he was hailed in Reykjavík as one of the saga lovers who had strengthened ties between the English and Norse. Subsequent to that visit, he published his translation of *Gisli the Outlaw* in 1866.

In 1870, he was appointed a civil service commissioner and consequently resigned his post at The Times. In 1876 he was knighted in England, though he was already a Danish knight.

Dasent retired from the public service in 1892 and died at Ascot in June 1896. He was survived by his wife, two sons, and a daughter, Frances Emily Mary. The younger son was Arthur Irwin Dasent and the elder son was Sir John Roche Dasent. Another son, George William Manuel Dasent, had previously drowned near Sandford-on-Thames.

Robert Hamill Nassau

Robert Hamill Nassau was born in 1835, and was an American presbyterian missionary who spent forty years in Africa.

Robert was born in Montgomery Square, Pennsylvania and went to the Lawrenceville School in Lawrenceville, New Jersey, continuing his education at the College of New Jersey. From 1856 to 1859 he moved on to the Princeton Theological Seminary and obtained a medical qualification from Pennsylvania Medical School in 1861.

On the instigation of the Presbytery of New Brunswick he joined the Presbyterian Board of Foreign Missions as a missionary, with his first posting being to the African island of Corisco. Throughout his career he served as a missionary in many places, including Benita; Belambla; Kangwe; Talaguga; Baraka, now Libreville, and Batanga. Nassau established a mission station in Lambaréné.

He returned to the USA in 1906 and settled in Florida.

Nassau's first wife was Mary Cloyd Latta, a fellow missionary who died on Corisco in 1870. They had three sons William Latta, George Paul and Charles Francis His second wife was Mary Brunette Foster, with whom he had a daughter Mary Brunette Foster.

Robert Hamill Nassau died in Ambler, Pennsylvania on May 6, 1921. His papers are kept as part of the Burke Library Archives, held at the Columbia University Libraries, New York.

Captain R. S. Rattray

Robert Sutherland Rattray, GBE, known as Captain R. S. Rattray, born in India in 1881, was a barrister and held a diploma in Anthropology from Oxford.

He was an early Africanist and student of the Ashanti. He was one of the early writers on Oware, and on Ashanti gold weights. An amusement park constructed by the Kumasi Metropolitan Assembly is named Rattray park as a memorial.

In 1906 he joined the Gold Coast Customs Service. In 1911 he became the assistant District Commissioner at Ejura. Learning local languages, he was appointed head of the Anthropological Department of Asante in 1921. He retired in 1930 and was killed while flying a glider in 1938.

"When a new Anthropological Department was set up in Ashanti in the 1920s, Rattray was charged with the task of researching the law and constitution of the Ashanti, to assist the colonial administrators in ruling the Ashantis. With his office in the Anthropological Department in Ashanti, Rattray set out to do detailed and voluminous research on Ashanti religion, customs law, art, beliefs, folktales, and proverbs. His personal contact with the people of Ashanti afforded him an intimate knowledge of their culture, which is reflected in his thoughtful and nuanced writing on them."*

* from *African Folklore: An Encyclopaedia*, by Philip M. Peek and Kwesi Yankah, New York & London: Routledge.

ABOUT THE EDITOR

I was born in 1962 into a predominantly sporting household – Dad being a good footballer, playing senior amateur and lower league professional football in England, as well as running a series of private businesses in partnership with mum, herself an accomplished and medal winning dancer.

I obtained a degree in History from Leeds University before wandering rather haphazardly into the emerging world of business computing in the late nineteen-eighties.

A little like my sporting father, I followed a succession of amateur writing paths alongside my career in technology, including working as a freelance journalist and book reviewer, my one claim to fame being a by-line in a national newspaper in the UK, The Sunday people.

I also spent 10 years treading the boards, appearing all over the south of the UK in pantos and plays, in village halls and occasionally on the stage of a professional theatre or two.

Following the sporting theme, and a while after I hung up my own boots, I worked on live TV broadcasts for the BBC, ITV, TVNZ, EuroSport and others as a rugby "Stato", covering Heineken Cups, Six Nations, IRB World Sevens and IRB World Cups in the late '90's and early '00's.

I try to combine my love of storytelling with a passion for information technology, working as a senior leader and investor in technology based businesses.

You can find out more about me at: www.boyonabench.com

ALSO BY CLIVE GILSON - *FICTION*

- Songs Of Bliss
- Out Of The Walled Garden
- The Mechanic's Curse
- The Insomniac Booth
- A Solitude Of Stars

AS EDITOR – *FIRESIDE TALES – Part 1, Europe*

- Tales From The Land Of Dragons
- Tales From The Land Of The Brave
- Tales From The Land Of Saints And Scholars
- Tales From The Land Of Hope And Glory
- Tales From Lands Of Snow And Ice
- Tales From The Viking Isles
- Tales From The Forest Lands
- Tales From The Old Norse
- More Tales About Saints And Scholars
- More Tales About Hope And Glory
- More Tales About Snow And Ice
- Tales From The Land Of Rabbits
- Tales Told By Bulls And Wolves
- Tales Of Fire & Bronze
- Tales From The Land Of The Strigoi
- Tales Told By The Wind Mother
- Tales From Gallia
- Tales From Germania

EDITOR – *FIRESIDE TALES – Part 2, North America*

- Okaraxta - Tales From The Great Plains
- Tibik-Kìzis – Tales From The Great Lakes & Canada
- Jóhonaa'éí –Tales From America's South West
- QugaaĝiX̂ - First Nation Tales From Alaska & The Arctic
- Karahkwa - First Nation Tales From America's Eastern States
- Pot-Likker - Folklore, Fairy Tales and Settler Stories From America

EDITOR – *FIRESIDE TALES – Part 3, Africa*

- Arokin Tales – Folklore & Fairy Tales from West Africa

Printed by BoD™in Norderstedt, Germany